GIRAFFE CARCASS

J. PETER W.

ATLATL

Atlatl Press
POB 521
Dayton, Ohio 45401
atlatlpress.com

GIRAFFE CARCASS

Also by J. Peter W.

For Carrie,
Thirteen years and counting . . .

ONE
LACEY

My mother was always beautiful. She made it seem effortless, even in death.

I can see the brush strokes on her forehead. The morticians went a little overboard on the makeup. I wish I was there to tell them there was no need for any. I would have left her pale and bloodless. That's how I remember her the last few weeks of her life.

I realize now the saying 'Cancer is a Bitch' is pretty accurate. I would add Motherfucking to it. Cancer is a Motherfucking Bitch.

I sit down on the pew next to Dad. He's staring at the floor, or at least it looks like it. I can tell from his expression his mind isn't here, just this shell of a body. He's been like that since he gave up. I follow his eyes to the burgundy carpet. Interwoven patterns of spiraling floral designs are spaced out every few feet.

His eyes are focused on one of the flowers, burning a hole into it.

Around me, wafts of heavy perfumes pass by as the air conditioning unit kicks on. It still doesn't hide the lingering stench of formaldehyde pumped into the flesh case that used to be my mother.

The preacher comes from behind us. "We're ready to start if you are."

Dad doesn't reply so I do it for him. "Yes." I look up just enough to make eye contact.

The preacher nods and goes to the back of the funeral parlor, opening the doors. I hear the shuffling of feet as the room fills with friends and family. I don't look back. I know they are all watching me, waiting for me to break down and cry, but I've already mourned. I don't have any more tears left to cry.

The funeral goes by in a flash. The preacher speaks and my Aunt Patty says a few things, it all just kind of blends together. The next thing I know the room is emptying and people are giving me hugs and telling me they're sorry.

It feels so staged, like I'm watching a television show.

Part of me wants to jump up and run around the room, telling everyone to stop acting like that. I want to grab them by the shoulders and shake them. I want to scream and wake up from this bad dream, but I can't even muster a mumble. Instead, I stand and walk outside, leaving my mother for the last time.

I'm so filled with anger I don't even realize it's raining until a man asks if I want his umbrella.

"Huh," I respond before feeling the droplets. "No thanks."

He walks away with a shrug and I suddenly feel cold and more alone than I have ever been in my entire life.

Behind me, Dad walks out of the funeral home and wrestles the keys from his trouser pocket. He unlocks the doors to the car and gets in the driver seat. I hesitate, letting the rain soak me for a few more seconds before getting in. We sit, neither one saying a word, listening to the raindrops smack the windshield. It's nice to have an outside noise fill our usual silence.

His arm finally lifts to the ignition. He makes it seem like even turning the key is an enormous chore. The car rumbles awake and he flicks on the wipers.

"They said she would be ready tomorrow. I guess I'll have to come back up here," he says as he puts the car in reverse.

"Where are we going to put her?"

"I'll keep her in my room for now."

"Isn't that a little weird?"

"Would you rather we put her on the mantle?"

I'm not sure if he is being sarcastic or not so I don't answer.

He glances at me before saying, "I think my room will be fine."

"Yeah, I guess."

I watch the rain bounce on the glass and I get thrown into a memory from a few years ago. Mom was healthy and Dad was alert. They were happy. I remember sitting at home by the window, watching the third day in a row of rain ruin my summer vacation. Behind me they danced to some '80s pop song. I always acted like it bothered me when they were goofing around like that, but honestly it made me smile.

"What's the long face for?" Mom asked. She left Dad hopping in the kitchen and came over to the window.

"Nothing."

3

She looked back at Dad and he hopped into the room.

"Is our little Lacey-boo upset?"

"Dad, no. Please don't call me that."

"She wants to go out. You want to go out, don't you?" Mom said.

I shrugged, but it was obvious.

"I've got an idea," Dad announced. Then he ran into the garage, leaving us there by the window.

Mom and I looked at each other, neither sure what Dad was up to. When he returned he had his old boom box and a handful of CDs.

"Let's take this dance party outside!"

"What?"

Mom stood up and grabbed my hand, pulling me up with her. "That sounds like fun. What do you say?"

"It's raining."

"Exactly," Dad replied. "Grab your boots and let's go."

Mom opened the coat closet and handed me a raincoat and my boots. She pulled out hers and Dad's as well. When we were coated and booted, we followed Dad out to the back porch. He placed the boom box down and loaded a disc into the player. Soon the sound of heavy rainfall was accompanied by blaring beats and synths. Melodies blasted out into the yard.

"May I have this dance?" Dad reached out a hand.

I clasped onto him, stepping from the safety of the porch and into the rain. Mom came right after, looking up into the sky as the droplets hit her face. She laughed and twirled around. Dad spun me and everything seemed right in the world.

We danced until our legs were tired and we were out of

breath, soaked and exhausted.

Dad pulls the car into the driveway and puts it in park. He sits for a second, staring at the garage door. The wipers swat away the rain to the beat of my memory song. I wait for him to say something, to try and comfort me. Instead, he exhales and turns the car off. I watch him step out into the rain.

I'm not sure I have the strength to follow him. Not that I want to spend the night in the car, but every movement feels like work. I close my eyes and will myself to get up.

When I get inside, Dad is hovering in the kitchen. He's looking at his phone, though he doesn't really seem to be doing anything particular on it. As soon as I get close to him he steps away and moves toward the stairs.

"I think there's some leftover pizza in the fridge," he says. "I'm gonna call it a night."

"It's three in the afternoon," I say, but he's already halfway up the stairs and doesn't hear me.

I open the fridge out of habit and see the pizza. My stomach is growling so I pull out the box and a soda. My arms feel weak just lifting them to the counter. After I eat maybe I should go lie down too.

Outside the rain is falling harder. I try not to find the irony.

I eat standing up, hoping to regain some energy instead of allowing the depression to swallow me whole. The pizza is rubbery but good. I eat two pieces before placing the box back in the fridge. We've been eating like this for a few weeks now. Dad was never much of a cooker; that was always Mom's field. I guess he'll have to learn. I guess we both will.

I mope into the living room and plop on the couch. Television feels like a chore, so I sit in silence, still listening to the heavy rain hitting the windows and the roof. Before long I'm daydreaming of the memory I had in the car, life before cancer. A happy mom and dad. All of us smiling like fools while the grim reaper peers from over our shoulders.

I should have known life couldn't be that good for long. Eventually something bad would have to happen. I just wish it wouldn't have been Mom. She was the heart of the family. And now that the heart is gone, Dad and I are just zombies wandering through life, slowly rotting away.

TWO
RICHARD

I feel like I'm learning to breathe again.

Every few seconds I consciously take in air and release it. It's like the part of my brain controlling all the mundane basic survival instincts has stopped working. I'm pretty sure I'm going to die from lack of oxygen if I don't remind myself to breathe.

That's what my life has come to: *concentrated breathing*.

My wife is dead. It still seems wrong saying it. I don't know if it will ever be right.

Kara was the only woman I ever loved. I can't see myself loving another. Maybe it's too soon to even try to comprehend something like that but deep down I know it's true. I will live out the rest of my days single, lost in the memories of my deceased wife. The weight of that idea rests heavily on my shoulders and I collapse in our—my—bed.

Even though I've been sleeping in the bed alone for several

weeks now, it's just now hitting me that I will be sleeping alone for the rest of my life. She isn't coming back. She'll never lay her head on the pillow again. She'll never snuggle up against me, entangling her limbs into mine.

I pull her pillow into my face, smelling her scent. It's already fading. I know that it too will be gone soon. I picture her in bed with me, smiling in that way that only she could, riding that line of bursting into laughter.

"Fuck." I need to stop. I can't live like this. I throw the pillow against the wall and stare up at the ceiling.

My lungs start to burn and I remember I need to breathe. Air in, air out, air in, air out.

THREE
LACEY

I wake up to the sound of my phone buzzing. It vibrates across the coffee table in the most annoying manner possible. It takes me a second to realize I fell asleep on the couch for a few hours. The whole house is dark.

I pick up my phone and see Renee is calling. I automatically take the call and instantly regret it when I remember that means talking and interacting with another person.

"Hello," I say and silently curse.

"Hey, Boo," she says.

"You know I hate that."

"Yeah, yeah. So, sorry I didn't stay long at the funeral. Dead people give me the creeps."

"It wasn't some random person, you know," I remind her.

"It didn't even look like your mom. It looked like some bad sculpture of her or something. No offense," Renee says.

"Yeah, I know what you mean."

"So is your dad like going psycho or something," she asks. "He was like totally staring off into space the whole time."

"He's been like that for a few weeks now. I don't know how long it's supposed to last." I rub my eyes and try to stand but my right leg is asleep. I stumble back onto the couch.

"Are you okay?" Renee asks.

"Fine. Did you want something?" The words come out harsher than I mean.

"Just seeing how you are. My mom asked me to call you, to be honest," Renee spit. "I won't bother calling again."

"Good. I'm fine. My dad is fine. Tell your mom we don't need any more check-ins."

Renee ends the call first, clicking off just as I finish speaking. I move the phone from my ear and look at the black screen, confirming the silence.

I place the phone back in my pocket and maneuver over to the light switch, flicking it on. The brightness temporarily blinds me, but I quickly adjust. The clock next to me indicates it's a little after nine, but it feels much later than that. I walk into the kitchen and find my warm, half-empty can of soda from that afternoon. I take a sip and dump the rest in the sink.

Outside the rain has stopped. I can see the moonlight reflecting off the wet grass as if the storm just ended recently. For a second I entertain the idea of going for a night walk. They used to be my favorite, but again my lack of energy overrides any contemplations of physical activity. Instead, I decide to go upstairs and lie down.

My room is on the opposite end of my parents—or rather, my

Dad's. I walk past his shut door and see nothing but blackness around the cracks. I picture him lying awake and staring at the dark ceiling. I'm not sure he'll ever be the same.

I flip on the light in my room and quietly shut the door. The bed is calling me but for some reason I drift to my desk. I plop on the seat in front of my laptop and click it awake. Before I realize what I'm doing I'm checking my social media pages and scrolling through emails. I hate how automatic it feels. Even after everything I've been through my brain still manages to focus on a mundane routine.

I see a few messages from acquaintances, the usual crap people say when a person dies. I can tell none of them have ever lost anyone close before. If they had they wouldn't be writing me the stereotypical apologies and condolences. Anyone who's lost someone they really cared about knows how useless it is to hear that.

I read a couple and get angry so I click out and shut my laptop. I need to escape from this for a while. I thought after the funeral I would be free from the stares and whispers and phony "I'm so sorry" stuff. I thought I would be able to just move on and forget.

I go to my closet and pull out some sweat pants and a t-shirt. I quickly change and toss my dirty clothes in the hamper. A box on the closet shelf catches my eye. It's filled with old junk that I can't seem to throw out. I know there are some pictures of Mom and me. I grab it and move to the bed. After a moment of hesitation, knowing the feelings that will follow from looking through it, I open the box.

On top there is a pile of photos that span most of my

childhood—fourteen years of happiness and one of confusion, depression, and anger. I pick up a handful and flip through them, watching my parents getting older, watching me getting taller. I realize how good I had it for most of my life. Seeing Mom and Dad smiling in the photos makes it impossible for me to hold back a smirk. It's just a twinkling of light in the darkness, but it makes me feel like things will be better one day. I will be able to get through this and live a normal life.

I set the photos to the side and see my old diary. The worn, brown leather cover is barely attached. I used to write in its innards daily. Some of the pages are just a single sentence, while others are covered in barely decipherable scribble. I can tell what my mood was at the time by the legibility of the writing.

I decide to lie down and read through it, relive the good ol' days.

A few pages in and I can picture myself at that age: a preteen, curious and naive. The world ahead of me without a clue of how to navigate it. By page ten I remember how close I used to be with my Dad. We watched movies and read books together. He would take me to concerts and games while Mom was working. He used to be so fun.

I turn to a page that has a rough sketch of what appears to be a castle. It looks like a poor man's version of the Disney castle, or at least a child's drawing of it. At first I'm baffled. I know I've never been there before and I don't remember ever having an affinity for it. On the back I see stick figure Dad and stick figure me holding hands and smiling. The next page I write about how my daddy promised me a castle. He told me he goes to work every day so he can save up enough money to buy me a castle. I couldn't wait until my birthday.

I nearly laugh out loud at how silly I was for believing him. I know now he was clearly just telling me what I wanted to hear so he could go to work without me whining. I was a gullible kid.

I suddenly feel battling emotions of sadness and happiness.

It's funny how a few years of growing up can change your perception of life.

I set the diary down on the bed and roll over on my side, closing my eyes. I'm unable to fight the exhaustion any more.

FOUR
RICHARD

No matter how hard I shut my eyes I can't escape the vision of my wife's face. It's not her smiling, happy, living face. All I can see is her death mask. It's haunting me.

I give up on sleep and stare at the ceiling. Shadows spread across from the partial moonlight that creeps through the blinds. I swear I see the shapes of dark fingers. It reminds me of the dark turn my life has taken. The disease that murdered my wife is holding me down in the blackness, filling me with it. I picture it seeping in through my eyes, mouth, and nose. I think of it like a smoke, flowing into my organs and suffocating them.

Toxic.

My whole being is toxic now.

I sit up, despite feeling like I could literally rot away in bed, and get to my feet. The only way to combat this dark disease is to move forward. I can't let it bury me as well.

I shuffle to the bathroom and lift the lid on the toilet. I piss a steady stream even though I can't remember drinking anything the entire day. The thought makes my mouth cotton-ball dry.

Fuck. I need coffee.

I flush and walk out of the bathroom, going straight to the door. I glance at the shadow hand on the ceiling, quickening my pace. Lacey's door is closed but the light is on. I check my watch. It's almost three in the morning. I consider knocking to see if she's still up. I take a step to her door and raise my arm but hesitate before knuckling it. I don't hear anything. She's probably asleep. I shouldn't wake her.

I go down the steps and walk into the kitchen. I look outside, noting the storm's end. Thin clouds cover half the moon, only partially obstructing the light. It's enough for me to navigate the coffee maker.

It feels wrong to turn on the lights so I just sit in the darkness, waiting for the brew to complete. As soon as the stream starts, the room fills with the scent of a roasted Colombian bean. I pour a cup, stir in some sugar, and sit back down at the table.

This is my life now, coffee conversations in my head. The thought of decades of this gives me a sinking feeling and I quickly pull myself up before I get too deep. The balancing act of it all would be a tricky motherfucker. I hope I learn the ropes sooner rather than later. I don't know if I can handle a lifelong battle like that.

The rest of the night drifts by in shifts of thoughtless zombie-mind chunks and waves of lucid daydreams of Kara. Before I know it the sun is shining through the windows, reminding me of the existence of the world outside my head. I recall the funeral home director telling me about picking up the urn.

What the fuck am I supposed to do with a vase filled with ashes? I know Kara wanted to be cremated but she never specified what she wanted done after that. I guess neither of us wanted to think about it.

FIVE
LACEY

Sunlight spreads across my room, piercing around the gaps of the window curtains. I open my eyes just enough to get blinded by the morning brightness and then quickly shut them. I was hoping a full night's rest would give me the energy to get through the day. I was optimistic that it would recharge me. One minute into this new day and I can tell the opposite has occurred. I feel even more exhausted. My body is aching.

I know the best way to get through this is to just sit up and muscle through it. Take one step at a time, put one foot in front of the other, or however that saying goes. But knowing how to get through it and actually proceeding forward with it are two very different things.

I focus my attention on a sound I hear downstairs. It's strangely familiar; a high-pitched clanking noise. I try to place it and realize it's the sound of a spoon stirring around the inside of a porcelain mug. That's followed by an amazing scent. Is that coffee?

I sit up immediately and take in a deep whiff. My eyes shoot open. It's been weeks since I've woken up to that smell.

I hop out of bed and go to the door. As soon as I open it I can see my dad's bedroom door is open. I see his bed is empty. I feel so suddenly filled with hope I nearly implode.

Daddy! I run down the stairs like a child on Christmas morning. I leap through the living room and slide into the kitchen. I see a fresh pot of coffee, the steam still rising. Then I hear the side door close.

I run to the window and see my dad getting in his car. I quickly fling the door open, but he's already backing out the driveway, completely unaware of me. At first my mind runs straight to him abandoning me, but I quickly reel it back in and tell myself there's a rational reason for him leaving.

I go back inside and move right to the coffee. I grab an oversized mug from the cabinet and fill it close to the top. Black isn't my favorite but I feel it's in order today. I dive right in, sipping it down despite its smoldering heat. The coffee tastes amazing, instantly warming my stomach. I close my eyes and savor it, leaning back against the counter.

When I open my eyes I look out over the backyard. I know right away that something is out of place but what I see is so obscure I hesitate to process it.

"What the hell?"

My fingers lose their strength and I drop the mug. It shatters on the floor, splashing hot coffee all over my legs. I don't react. I'm stuck in a frozen stare. Lying out in my very suburban, fenced-in backyard is an enormous body. I recognize the type of body it is but it doesn't make sense. A giraffe? Here? In my yard?

I step out of the puddle of coffee and mug shards, leaving them there as I move to the back door. I'm nearly certain the body will disappear when I open the door. I must be hallucinating. But as soon as I open it I can see the giraffe is still there, just lying on the grass.

"Is it sleeping?" I ask out loud, half hoping someone will be there with it.

I try to rationalize. I'm going through multiple scenarios of how it could possibly be in my backyard. I guess it could've escaped from the zoo. But then I think about how far I live from the zoo; that would be like a two-day walk. There's no way it would have gotten this far without someone seeing it. Maybe it was being transferred on a train or a tractor trailer. Maybe the truck wrecked and the giraffe escaped. Maybe there are more animals out there, lying in my neighbors' backyards. I look around but none of the other yards look occupied by a large exotic animal.

I step down off the back porch and into the wet grass. My eyes lock onto the giraffe. With each step I take, the more I can see. Its fur looks muddled and its skin seems decrepit. When I get about ten feet away the smell hits me and I realize it's dead. Well, not just dead but rotten, long-dead rotten. I move closer to its head and see the giraffe's face. The eyes are gone, sunken in, revealing its skull. Multiple areas around its mouth have rotted away as well, making the thing's large teeth easily visible, prodding from dark gums like gravestones. A purple, slug-like tongue is splayed out over its bottom jaw.

"Gross," I mutter and turn away, trying my best not to vomit.

I look around the yard for a break in the fence but there's nothing. No giraffe footprints or human footprints, no tire marks, nothing. The giraffe's clearly been dead for several days and I'm pretty sure I didn't see it in the yard yesterday. How did it get here? It doesn't make any sense.

The wind kicks the rotten smell directly in my face and I nearly vomit again. I decide to go back in the house and wait for Dad. He's not going to believe this.

I clean up the coffee and porcelain pieces from the kitchen floor and pour myself another cup, this time sitting down at the table so I don't drop it again. I'm only sitting for a few minutes when Dad gets home. He's holding my mom's ashes in a chrome urn when he walks in the side door.

"Got her," he says, setting the urn down on the kitchen counter.

I guess he sees the crazed expression on my face because he immediately asks, "Are you okay? What's going on?"

All I can do is point.

"What is it? Something in the backyard? This is the last thing we need. If someone is—" He stops mid-sentence when he sees the giraffe carcass.

"Yep. That was my reaction too," I finally say.

"What is that? Is it real?" he asks.

"It was."

He turns his head and looks at me. "Was?"

"It's dead. A real, dead giraffe in our backyard."

"But how? When did—? Who would have—?" He can't seem to complete a thought.

"I have no idea."

He sets the urn on the table in front of me and goes to the back door. I follow him, staying on the porch as he circles the carcass much like I did earlier. He looks around the yard. I'm guessing he's surveying the fence and the grass, looking for some sort of explanation.

When he looks back at me I can only shrug and shake my head.

"We have to call the police or . . . someone," he says as he makes his way back in the house.

He goes right to his cell phone and I go right back to my coffee.

He calls the police first and then animal control after the operator advises him to. I can tell both the police operator and the animal control administrator are having a hard time believing him. I nearly spit my coffee everywhere and laugh out loud when he says "Giraffe, like the god damn Toys 'r' Us mascot!"

When he finally gets off the phone we are both smiling like over-medicated lunatics. At least we're smiling today.

SIX
RICHARD

If Lacey wasn't here seeing the same crazy shit I was seeing, I'd be certain I was a goner: a full-blown psychotic, imagining large dead animals in my backyard. But she's here. She's seeing the same thing. Maybe we are both goners.

This is the last thing I need.

I grab the urn off the kitchen table and go upstairs. I set it on the dresser and pace my room, hoping I don't come across like a man unwinding at the seams when the police arrive. I try to calm the whirring sounds of fighting voices in my head. I can't seem to concentrate on any one idea. Everything feels like chaos. I keep picturing a dark room with a string dangling from a light bulb. My hands stretch out, fumbling around it, unable to grasp hold of it. It's like a hologram. A ghost string.

Focus. Calm down.

I sit on the edge of the bed and close my eyes.

The police will know what to do. Why am I even stressing about this? This will soon be their problem and one less weight on my shoulders.

I suddenly hear a scratching sound. It's like fingernails on metal. My eyes dart to the urn. Then I hear it again. I step up to it and put my ear against the side.

It happens again. My eyes open wide, terrified.

There. Is. No. Fucking. Way.

SEVEN
LACEY

About twenty minutes later the police get to the house first. It's a deputy riding solo. He pulls into the driveway slowly, no lights shining or sirens blaring. I watch him from the living room window as he gets out of his car, adjusting his belt as he stands up. He says something into a walkie-talkie attached to his shoulder before coming up to the door.

"The police are here!" I shout to Dad.

"Finally," he says from upstairs. "Let them in."

I open the door just as the officer is stepping onto the front porch. Dad bounces down the stairs.

"I got a call about an animal in your backyard," the deputy says. I can tell he is being coy with us.

"A giraffe," I reply, reading the name on his badge. "Deputy Thompson." I emphasize the silent H and the silent P. It makes me sound like I have a lisp. I'm not sure why I did it.

"A dead one," Dad adds.

"Is that right?" the officer says. "Well, lead the way."

We bring him in through the house and immediately he is scanning the rooms suspiciously. I guess that's just a natural cop thing. I don't understand how the inside of our house would have anything to do with a giraffe carcass outside. All three of us go into the backyard, although Deputy Thompson stops just a few steps in.

"Holy shit!"

"Told you," I say.

"You weren't joking, were you," Deputy Thompson replies. "That's a real motherfucking giraffe."

Dad and I exchange glances.

"Oh, uh, sorry about my language, but dang, I have never, in all my days, seen anything like that."

"It's understandable. We have no idea how it got here," Dad tells him.

The deputy walks over to the carcass and circles it. He sticks his leg out and gives the giraffe's chest a nudge with his boot. "Just woke up and saw this in your backyard," he says. "I'd be pretty shocked myself."

"Yeah, I guess shocked is the word. Baffled, shocked, perplexed," Dad starts rambling.

Deputy Thompson ignores my dad and goes to his walkie-talkie. "Do we have a 10-20 on the animal control unit?"

A static-filled voice replies something I can barely make out.

"I'm gonna need a long bed 11-85 here, maybe a crane. We got one hell of a 10-91D. I'll let AC make the call on that."

I look at Dad to see if he understands the code words but he seems just as clueless as me.

When the officer is done talking to the operator he turns back to us. "We're gonna have this mess out of here soon enough. Just bear with us while we figure out the best way to go about it."

"Sure, sure," Dad replies.

Deputy Thompson then walks to the fence gate and goes into the front yard. Dad sits down on the porch steps and pats a spot beside him.

"What do you think Mom would be saying right now?" I ask him as I sit down.

"I don't know if she would be laughing or crying."

"Or both," I add.

"Yeah," Dad chuckles before staring off into space again.

I shouldn't have mentioned Mom. He was acting normal, well, as normal as someone with a dead giraffe in his backyard, but now he's gone. Lost in the memories and sadness and depression again.

"Dad?"

He stands up and goes to the back door. "I think I'm gonna go in for a bit. Let me know if the officer needs anything."

"Dad?"

He closes the door, ignoring me.

When the deputy returns, he is accompanied by two other men. They all start laughing when they see the giraffe. It ends up taking hours for them to figure out a way to remove the carcass. At first they try and drag it with a tow truck, but the ropes end up cutting through it more than moving it. Next, they bring in a crane and try to lift it onto the tow truck, but again the flesh of the rotten carcass isn't strong enough to withstand the ropes. It breaks into chunks. Finally, just before the sun begins setting, they are able to come up with a way to get it out of the yard.

They take down part of our fence and drive in a tractor with a front loader. Once the tractor gets back there it doesn't take long for them to scoop up the remains and drop them into a dump truck. It feels like the failed attempts and preparation wasted so much time. If someone would have thought of the tractor at first, it could have been done in a couple of hours and not an entire day.

Dad comes out when they are finishing up and speaks with Deputy Thompson, thanking him and everyone else. I'm assuming he was watching from the window in his room, waiting for them to remove it so he could get back to his depressed moping.

"That was a mess," I say to him as he heads back inside.

"Yep."

I follow him into the house as the officer and the other men drive away. It's still hard to believe we had a giraffe in the backyard.

Throughout the day, several neighbors peeped over, talking to one of the workers or the police. I'm sure the entire subdivision is buzzing with the story. It's just another reason for me to hide inside and avoid them all from now on.

Dad goes right to the stairs again, halfway up before I'm even in the door.

"What's for dinner? Two-day-old pizza?" I ask.

"I don't know, Lacey. I'm sure there's something in there. If you want to walk to the corner store and get a sandwich or whatever, that's fine. I think there's a few bucks in my jacket pocket." He says all this while going up the stairs, closing the door to his room just as he finishes.

I feel like screaming.

I stomp into the kitchen and dig out the cash from his jacket. I go out the side door, slamming it behind me. I want him to know I'm pissed. I want him to feel guilty or angry, or anything. Just feel something. Wake up!

EIGHT
RICHARD

"Kara?"

The scratching sound stops as I pick up the urn.

"Richard!"

Fuck. I drop it and fall backward, sliding across the beige carpet, pushing myself back into the corner. I pull my knees up in front of my face, peeking out just above them. The urn is lying on its side, thankfully still closed.

"Is this real? Are you really talking to me?" I say after several minutes of silence.

"Richard, you can hear me!" The voice is hers, Kara's. Somehow it's emanating from the urn filled with her ashes.

I think I'm losing it. I think I've finally walked off the deep end, limbs locked, floating down into the darkness without a clue in which direction to swim.

"Kara? I'm here. I can hear you." My voice is trembling and

unsure. I lift my head higher, no longer hiding behind the safety of my knees.

"Come and hold me. I miss you," she says.

I don't hesitate. I crawl over and snatch the urn up in my arms, hugging it like I would if it was her physical body. Tears roll down my cheeks. I embrace my insanity.

NINE
LACEY

It's pretty much dark when I get outside. A small strip of deep orange is lingering in the distance, but otherwise the sky is purple and filled with stars. I'm only two steps onto the street when I see someone riding a bike up ahead of me. They seem to be angling right toward me.

"Shit," I mumble when I recognize who it is.

"Hey, Boo."

"Renee."

She rides past me and then circles around. She takes her feet off the pedals and walks her bike on my left side.

"Heard about the giraffe. That's crazy. How in the heck did it get there?"

"I don't know. No one does. It's a mystery," I tell her.

"So you didn't see it walk back there?"

"Nope." I start to walk faster, not so much to get away from her, more so to make it difficult for her to keep up.

"My mom says your dad is losing it and he probably put it there," Renee says. She's already breathing heavy from walking the bike at a faster speed.

"Your mom doesn't have a clue."

"Everyone is talking about it. They say he's going to snap soon and end up hurting himself and you."

"He would never hurt me," I say. "Your mom really needs to keep her nose out of our business."

Renee gets up on her bike, pedaling now. "A dead giraffe in our neighborhood is our business, okay? It's everyone's business, especially if your dad is going crazy and putting dead things everywhere."

She turns around and quickly rides away before I can reply.

"Bitch." I nearly yell it, but hold back, realizing after our conversation that the neighbors are watching me. There are probably multiple sets of eyes on me right now. No need to add to the lie that my dad and I are losing it.

When I get to the corner store it's full dark outside and I realize I'm wearing all black. The perfect camouflage for someone trying to stay invisible. I cautiously walk across the parking lot and up to the door. There are a couple of people inside, none of them I recognize except for Tony, the cashier. He nods a greeting and then goes right back to his phone. We've done this exchange weekly for over a month now. It usually involves me being here alone, trying to balance buying enough food and drink to last for a few days and not getting too much to carry back home.

I load up my arms and struggle to get to the register. Tony

smirks as I reach the counter and the groceries fall across it.

"That everything?" he jokes.

"Just ring me up," I reply.

"I heard about the——"

"Don't." I cut him off before he can even come close to saying the word giraffe.

Both hands shoot up as if he's surrendering to me, pausing there a few seconds too long. Finally, he starts to ring up the items. I wonder if I came off too harsh. He was clearly just trying to get a conversation going. The problem is that it's the same conversation every time, excluding the giraffe, of course. I wish he would just ask me for my number or stop the small talk altogether. I'm not much for the game, especially since my mom got sick. Not that I can picture us being together. He's cute and all, really nice eyes, but I just don't have room for a boyfriend in my life right now.

"Thirty-eight sixty-seven," he says, going into business mode and putting the groceries into plastic bags.

I pull out the two twenties I got from my dad's pocket and hand them over, avoiding eye-contact while doing so. When he hands me the change I glance quickly at his face before he can look at me and then right down to the counter.

"Thanks," I say. "See you next week."

I grab the bags and shuffle outside. The darkness of the night engulfs me as I leave the light shining through the glass front of the corner store. I instantly feel like I can breathe again. Night walks are my favorite thing in the whole world, I decide at that moment. There isn't a car in sight. I feel alone and isolated, and it helps me to forget how screwed up life has been lately.

It takes me nearly twice as long to get home as it took me to get to the store. I mosey my way back, not having to worry about annoying Renee chatting away beside me. I don't know what has been her problem lately. We used to be friends when we were younger but drifted a little in middle school. Last year was our first year of high school and it seemed like she just decided to turn into a total bitch. The timing of it coinciding with my mom getting sick pretty much turned me off from her forever.

I keep trying to let her know I don't want anything to do with her but she just isn't getting the hints, either that or she just likes messing with me. I wonder if it's going to take me being direct with her in order to get the point across. I'm going to have to just tell her straight up that I don't want to talk to her anymore and hope that does the trick.

Before I know it I'm back in front of my house. All the lights are off both inside and out. I guess Dad went to sleep already. Sometimes I wonder if he is trying to give me a hint.

I go in through the side door and set the bags on the floor. I glance out the back window and make sure we don't have any more unwanted visitors lingering around back there. The yard is clear of all animal carcasses and nosy neighbors, so I turn on the kitchen light and start putting the food away. I leave out a jar of peanut butter and the bread. At this point I just want something quick and easy to eat.

I make my sandwich and grab a bottle of water. I sit at the kitchen table overlooking the backyard through sheer curtains. Once again my mind is on the giraffe. There must be a logical explanation for it. There has to be. I wonder if giraffes are ever transported by plane. It could have fallen from a plane and landed in the backyard, but it was definitely rotten for days so it had to be from a plane transporting dead animals. If that kind of thing exists.

I convince myself that's the most probable explanation since I can't think of anything else that makes any sense at all. Whatever happened, it was pretty bizarre that it happened the day after my mom's funeral.

My mind meanders back to the funeral. I'm face-to-face with the thing that was supposedly my mom lying in the casket. It wasn't her; it was a terrible representation at best. I don't want to think about her like that. I want to remember her laughing and happy.

I finish up the last bite of my sandwich and then chug the remnants of the water before tossing the bottle in the trash. It's not even eight o'clock yet but I decide to go up to bed. I still can't handle television and I just want to put another day behind me.

TEN
RICHARD

I grab the urn and lie down on the floor in my dark bedroom. I put the thing holding my dead wife's ashes close to my chest. I can feel her presence in it. I can feel her with me, holding me too. It's both beautiful and terrifying at the same time.

"Will you always be here?" I ask.

Kara's voice lifts from the urn, not as if she is inside, but as if she is the urn itself. "I hope so," she says.

"I don't know what I'm doing without you."

"I'm here now, that's all that matters."

I hear Lacey come home, the door opening and shutting downstairs. The house is so quiet. She lingers in the kitchen, I assume preparing food. Part of me wants to rush down there and tell her about Kara. Let her know her mother is still here, somehow communicating from her ashes, but I know I can't. I know how crazy I am for even believing it's true. Instead, I sit up, lifting the urn with me, and get into bed. I want to remember what it's like to be with her again, to sleep with her in our bed.

ELEVEN
LACEY

The next morning I wake up to the same sunlight blinding me as the day before, realizing I never adjusted the curtains. I sniff the air, hoping to have a repeat of coffee goodness, but there isn't even the tiniest whiff of it. I check my clock and see it's just after seven-thirty. My body is begging me to stay in bed, feeling almost more tired than when I lay down last night, but my mind is already awake and bored.

I sit up and go to the bathroom, peeing, brushing my teeth, and then jump in the shower. The warm water helps my aching body. I realize I sound like an old lady every time I refer to my body as aching but that's how it feels. I remind myself not to mention aching out loud to anyone.

When I'm finished showering I wrap myself in a towel and stare into the fogged mirror. I wipe my hand across it, clearing off a section so I can see my face. I try to smile but it looks so forced it comes off more like a crazy person than a happy person. I wonder if Renee and her mom are right about us. Maybe we are losing it.

I dry off a little more before opening the door to go back to my room. Just as I'm about to open the door I stop and turn to the window. I lift up two slats on the blinds and peer into the backyard.

"Dad! Dad!" I shout. "It's back!"

Sure enough, lying in the exact same spot as last time is another giraffe, or maybe the same giraffe. How is this happening? One day of finding a giraffe carcass in your backyard has got to be incredibly rare, but two days, back-to-back is pretty much impossible.

I run out of the bathroom and collide with my dad's bedroom door.

"Dad!" I shout as I open it.

He's lying on top of the blanket, still fully dressed in yesterday's clothes. In his right arm, cradled next to him on the bed, is Mom's urn.

"What's wrong?" he asks.

"The dead giraffe," I say, panicky, "it's back. Or another one came. I don't know. Either way, there's another giraffe in the backyard!"

"What?" He rolls out of bed, leaving the urn there, and goes to the window, drawing up the blinds and leaning into the glass.

"See?"

"But how? Two days?" he says, unable to comprehend.

"What are we gonna do?"

He lets the blinds fall, ignoring me as he brushes past. I

haven't seen him move this quickly in months. I look back in his room, wondering why he was sleeping with the urn. I don't think it's healthy for him to be lying in bed with her ashes like that. I know I will have to bring it up later. I turn and follow him down the stairs.

When I get to the living room, Dad is already out back, once again circling the giraffe. He's scratching his head as if some stimulation will cause him to come up with an explanation that no one has thought of yet. I go to the door but stay just inside. I can't believe my eyes. It looks identical to the other, just as dead and just as rotten. None of it makes sense.

Dad comes back to the porch. The expression on his face is a mix of fear and trepidation. It's like he realizes he's in over his head.

"What do we do?" I ask him when he comes back inside.

"I guess we call the police again. I don't know what else we can do."

It suddenly hits me that the entire neighborhood is going to hear about it again. I'm never going to live this down. Whenever anyone sees me in school they are going to associate me with dead giraffes. My life is completely over.

"Do we have to?" I ask him as he pulls out his phone.

He starts dialing the non-emergency police. "Yes."

"Dad, everyone's going to think we're crazy."

He hushes me as the operator picks up. This time when he explains it the humor is gone. There is nothing funny about it anymore. Now it's become a nuisance, a burden he doesn't have the patience for. I go upstairs and get dressed while he gives our address to the operator.

When I come back down I see Dad standing outside with Deputy Thompson. The officer looks like he is scolding my dad. The conversation gets a little heated and I wonder if he is going to arrest my dad. I'm not sure what the charge would be. It's not like we put the giraffe there. Then I realize maybe that's what the cop is thinking. Maybe he is trying to figure out how and why my dad would have done it. I guess when there is no easy explanation they just have to make one up. I'm sure our neighbors are putting pressure on Deputy Thompson to figure it out.

I step outside and their conversation ends immediately. Obviously they don't want me to hear whatever it was about.

"Hey," I say.

Neither replies to me. Dad goes back inside, nearly bumping into me, and Deputy Thompson walks to the front yard.

"Or not."

I walk around to the front, following the officer, mainly to get away from the smell of the rotten carcass. As I come around I see the same tractor as last time rolling down the road. Behind it, a dump truck is following. I wonder where they dumped the one from yesterday. I wonder if they even had time to dump it.

All the neighbors are out in their front yards, some gathering together to spread more rumors, I assume. I see them staring at me. A couple are pointing. I know what they're thinking. No, I'm not in danger. I want to scream it out, but think better of it when I see Deputy Thompson watching me.

I wave a hand and this time he nods before looking down the road at the oncoming tractor.

I move to the back porch when they get here. They've

obviously gotten the hang of giraffe carcass removal because they get the thing up in one piece and out of our yard in just a few minutes.

The neighborhood echoes with a crunching splash when the tractor drops the rotten body into the dump truck. I hear it from the backyard.

"Tell your father I don't want to have to come here again tomorrow," Deputy Thompson tells me. "I've got my eye on him."

"We didn't have anything to do with it," I say. "It just appeared."

"Once and I would believe you," he replies. "Twice and that's no coincidence, young lady. Your father has been through a lot and I wouldn't put anything past him. You need to be watching your back."

"I don't think—"

"Here," he cuts me off, handing me a business card. "Call me directly if he starts acting strangely. I'll be here any time, day or night, okay?"

I take the card and nod, just wanting the conversation to end, then go inside. I can't take another minute of my neighbors' staring at me with both pity and bafflement. I'm fine, people. Get a life.

TWELVE
RICHARD

After I get off the phone with the operator I feel like a huge failure. I hate dumping things on people, but I've got too many problems right now. Figuring out how to get rid of a giant, rotting animal seems impossible. I step outside, hoping the police hurry and get here. The smell of the rotten flesh is starting to seep into the house.

I see Deputy Thompson pull in the driveway and wave to him like he's an old pal. He doesn't return the greeting. I can tell right away he's all business today.

"Did I hear my operator correctly?" he belches out with a firm voice, eyes drilling holes right through my skull. He steps out of the car and starts toward me.

I nod. "Yeah."

"You're telling me there's another goddamn giraffe in your backyard?"

"Yep."

Deputy Thompson stops just on the edge of my comfort zone when it comes to personal space from strangers. I instinctively take a step backward.

He raises an incriminating finger, pointing it at my face and says, "And you had nothing to do with this?"

"Yeah, I don't know—"

"That's a tough pill to swallow." He steps around me and goes over to the giraffe. He slowly circles it, just like the day before.

"We just woke up and it was here," I tell him.

"This looks like the exact same corpse. It's the same size, in the same damn spot, with the same goddamn stench."

I walk up next to him. "It's pretty crazy, isn't it?"

His eyes move to mine. "Do you think I'm some kind of a moron?"

"No, of course not."

"Then why are you bullshitting me?"

"I'm telling you the truth. I don't know how it got here. I don't know why there's a dead giraffe in my backyard two days in a row," I say. I feel like I'm on the brink of breaking down. I need to get away from him before I lose it.

The back door opens and Lacey comes out. I take it as my cue to end the conversation and go back inside.

THIRTEEN
LACEY

When I go inside I'm surprised to see Dad standing in the kitchen. I'm so used to being alone downstairs that he almost looks out of place. Although, I quickly notice he seems even more defeated than usual, staring at the floor like it holds the answers to everything.

"The police seem suspicious of you. The whole neighborhood really," I tell him.

"Deputy Thompson let me know," he replies.

"That's ridiculous, isn't it?"

He smirks. "Of course."

"I got some sliced turkey and a loaf of bread last night. Do you want a sandwich?" I ask, moving to the refrigerator.

"No, thanks," Dad says.

"You have to eat." I pull out the turkey and set it on the counter. "Let me make it for you."

"I'm fine. You go on and eat. I just need to lie down for a bit."

"Dad, have you had anything to eat since the funeral?"

"I'm okay, really. I just need a few days to get my head straight. Everything will be fine," he says as he starts to walk away.

"This isn't the way to deal with it," I tell him. "We should be grieving together." My words fall on deaf ears. He's once more cocooning himself away from the world. Away from me.

I grind my teeth and pull out the bread. I don't know how I'm supposed to get through to him if he keeps hiding. This shouldn't be falling to me. He's the adult here. I'm supposed to be the one falling apart. I should be the one refusing to deal with the loss. How did I get stuck losing my mom and having to deal with a dad that can't cope?

I suddenly fill with anger; raw, overflowing, unhinged anger. I scream as loud as I can and start grabbing the wine glasses hanging from under the cabinets. Without giving it much thought, I begin slamming them to the floor, shattering glass everywhere. I run through five of them before I break into an enraged crying fit that shakes my whole body. My shoulders bounce uncontrollably. Tears pour down my face like I've been storing up gallons over the duration of my life.

I fall to the floor, barely avoiding glass shards, and weep for ten minutes.

When my whimpering slows to a sniffle, I wipe away the streaks of tears from my face and eyes. Snot and mucus bubble over my lips and chin. I swipe my sleeve across my mouth. I finally stand back up and step through the broken glass. I take the broom from the closet and start sweeping up the pieces. As good as it felt to throw them down, the short-lived satisfaction from seeing and hearing them break has already worn off and I'm left with nothing but guilt for destroying my mom's wine glasses.

I wonder if Dad even acknowledged it. I wonder if he even thought for a millisecond that I needed him down here. I doubt it. He probably didn't even think twice about it, if he even heard it to begin with. He is so lost in his own world right now.

A deeper layer of depression engulfs me. It's dark and heavy. It feels like it's too much for one person to take and I wonder how long I'll be able to hold on. I decide to turn my focus to the giraffe carcass situation before I give myself a full-blown panic attack.

Outside the air is breezy and light and I feel like I can breathe again. I close my eyes for a second and take a deep breath, holding it in for a bit. When I exhale I try to release all of my stresses with it. When I open my eyes I see the flattened grass where the giraffes were lying. The rest of the yard is covered in tractor tread marks. Divots and bare spots are scattered everywhere. I walk over the flattened grass and examine the ground.

"What the hell is going on?" I say it louder than I mean to, in reference to both the giraffes and my life as a whole.

"How are you holding up?" A voice startles me.

I turn around and see my neighbor, Ms. Plume, peeking over the five-foot fence.

"Oh, hey, I'm doing alright, I guess," I tell her.

We've only spoken a handful of times alone. My mom used to

have twenty-minute conversations with her every few days. They would talk about everything from cooking to gardening. Those are the parts I caught anyway.

"I miss her," she says.

"Me too." I look at the ground, digging my shoe into the dirt.

There is a hesitation in the conversation and I wonder if I should just walk away. It gets to the point of feeling awkward and I start to turn just as she speaks.

"Your mother told me something a little ..." Ms. Plume pauses midway through her statement while I look back, "odd the last time I spoke with her."

I think back to the last time Mom was feeling well enough to be outside. It seems like a lifetime ago.

"What did she say?"

Ms. Plume looks past me. I follow her eyes to the spot in the middle of the yard where the grass is flattened and the air still has the slightest linger of a day old carcass.

"She said that the first time the cancer struck her she got so close to dying that she began to have visions of death. She said it was as clear as watching television. It kept her up at night, haunting her," Ms. Plume tells me. "She said she was too terrified to tell you or your father, but she had to tell someone. I guess that someone was me."

I can see the fear in her eyes. "What did she see? Her own death?"

"She said she saw dead bodies everywhere, saw them starting in spurts, walking among the living until they've piled up, overwhelming us all," Ms. Plume says. Her voice is shaky as she speaks. "She said it would start with the animals."

I stare at her eyes. She seems genuine, or at least believes her own words. I'm not sure I'm on board though. "Zombies?" I ask.

"When she was telling me I thought the cancer had gotten to her mind. It wasn't until yesterday when I saw the giraffe that I thought about it again. And then after this morning, I don't know," she says. "I just wanted to tell you. I don't know what to believe. I'm sorry. I'm so sorry for everything."

I watch as Ms. Plume walks away, moving much faster than I have ever seen her walk. She goes into her house, shutting the door behind her, leaving me out here alone to process everything she just told me.

"What?" I say out loud. I'm not sure if she's the one who lost her mind or if it was my mom. Maybe it's just me. I nearly laugh out loud at the idea.

FOURTEEN
RICHARD

I walk into my room and see Kara—the urn still lying on the bed. I shut the door behind me and lie down next to her. I want to tell her everything. I want to tell her how much I miss her, tell her I'm struggling to survive without her, but most of all I want to tell her about the dead giraffes in the backyard.

"Kara?" I whisper.

"Yes, Richard. I'm here," her voice emanates from the urn. She sounds fragile and soft. I want to scoop her into my arms and hold her.

"I don't think I can continue on without you."

Her voice soothes me. "You must."

"But I need you. I can't do this on my own," I say.

"I'm here, Richard. Whenever you need me, I'll be right here."

"It's not the same. I can't hold you. I can't be with you."

She goes quiet. I wonder if she is thinking, pondering a deep thought. Then my mind goes paranoid and I immediately think she left, or maybe she was never here.

"It's starting already," she finally says.

"What's starting?"

"I knew it was coming. I thought you'd have more time to prepare."

I sit up in the bed and lift the urn, standing it upright. "What are you talking about?" I ask her.

"I had visions of this. There will be more. Lots more," she says.

"But, how am I supposed to get rid of them. The police think I'm responsible. They think I'm somehow putting them back there. I can't call the cops anymore. I have to figure out a way to get rid of them alone."

"No," she says sternly. "You will need them."

"Need them? The carcasses?"

"Yes."

FIFTEEN
LACEY

When I get back in the house I start pacing the living room without even realizing it. In my head the conversation with Ms. Plume is looping over and over again. No matter how hard I try I can't seem to picture my mother out there by the fence telling her about a zombie uprising. It sounds like a bad joke.

The rest of the day goes by in a blur and I have nothing to show for it besides a headache from the inability to wrap my mind around anything that's happening to me. As the sun starts to set, I fill with anxiety. I know when the dark arrives so does the unknown of tomorrow. What if another dead giraffe shows up? What if more animals show up? What if Ms. Plume's story about my mom was true and, even more so, what if my mom was right? Are zombies going to be running around the street?

I go upstairs and stop at my Dad's room. The door is slightly ajar, enough for me to peek inside. He's lying under the covers, lightly snoring. Mom's urn is still in the bed.

I go in my room, quickly realizing my anxiety isn't going to let me sleep tonight, and I come up with an idea. I decide to set up camp by my bedroom window. If another giraffe carcass shows up overnight then I'm going to see how it gets here.

I pull my desk chair over to the window and set my pillow on it so I can be comfortable. I pull the blinds up on the window and position myself so I can see the backyard unobstructed. There's no way a giraffe or, more likely, someone dropping off a rotten giraffe is going to get by me.

Before it gets too late I run back downstairs and get a bottle of water and a bag of chips. I decide against television and games. I want my full attention on the backyard so I don't miss it. When I get back in my seat, I open the chips and start chomping away, staring at the grass like a madman. I wonder if the neighbors can see me. I'm sure most of them already think I'm crazy.

The hours creep by and before I know it I'm battling to keep my eyes open. The fear and anxiety can only pump you up so much before your body starts to crash back down to reality. For me it only takes a few hours. It's barely after midnight and I'm falling asleep already.

"Wake up! Wake up!" I tell myself, slapping my cheeks to get some kind of stimulation.

It works for only a few minutes. After that I'm right back to fighting my eyelids. They feel heavy and weak and keeping them open seems impossible.

"You're going to miss it."

I finally stand up and shake out my limbs. I move to the center of my room and do some jumping jacks until I feel my blood flowing again.

My eyes survey the room, looking for anything that might help this unwinnable battle.

"Music! Yes, music," I say out loud. I grab my iPod and headphones and go back to my seat to make sure the backyard is still corpseless.

Once I'm sitting down, I crank the music as loud as I can handle it to upbeat dance hits; it's my cleaning playlist. I go back to the bag of chips and grab another handful even though I'm not hungry. The crunching helps massage my head and keep me awake, but even that can only help for so long. Within thirty minutes I pass out, dumping the bag of chips all over my lap.

When I wake up I'm still wearing my headphones, though I hear nothing but silence coming from them. I check my iPod. Dead battery. I rub my eyes and stretch my arms before I remember I was keeping watch on the backyard. I sit up in my chair, immediately checking the spot in the yard where the other carcasses were lying.

"How the hell?" The words fall from my mouth.

Lying in the backyard, in the exact same spot as the two previous mornings, is another dead giraffe. I blink my eyes in a quick flutter and then begin rubbing them again, hoping it's just a delusion.

"I need to tell Dad. He's going to freak out," I say. "This is ridiculous."

I stand up and leave my room, walking up to his closed bedroom door. It's well after noon already, but I know he's still sleeping. I take a deep breath before knocking.

"Dad? Dad?" I call out as I tap the door with my knuckles.

"You awake yet?"

I hear the covers rustling around and the bed creak before he answers with a groggy, incoherent moan.

I open the door slowly. "Dad?"

"Yeah. What's wrong? What happened?" he asks.

"There's another one."

"Giraffe?"

"Yes." I almost laugh at how silly it is. "Should I call the police again?"

"No, no-no," he says, sitting up. "We can't."

"They think you're the one doing it," I say.

"It seems that way. I would too if I were them."

"So what do we do?"

"I'll take care of it," he replies. "I'll be down in a few minutes."

I shut his door and go down the stairs, trying to imagine how he is going to take care of it. We don't have a tractor or a tow truck. We don't even have a pickup truck. How is he planning to move the thing?

I go into the kitchen and get a glass of water, staring at the carcass through the window above the sink. My eyes drift to the fence where I spoke with Ms. Plume. I wonder if she's seen the giraffe yet.

I hear Dad stomping down the stairs and turn to see him. He has a strange look in his eyes. It's a mix of anger and bewilderment. He walks through the kitchen without saying a word to me and goes right outside.

"Dad?" I call after but the door closes behind him. A chill runs through me from the bottom of my back to the tips of my fingers. I have a feeling this isn't going to be good.

I follow Dad outside, staying on the porch while he goes into the shed. The door swings closed behind him and I can't tell what he's doing. When he reappears he has an ax in his hand. I'd forgotten we even had one. I'm pretty sure it was a hand-me-down from an older relative. It looks ancient. The wood is cracked and splintered and the head is rusted and dented.

He glances over, finally acknowledging me, but then turns his eyes to the carcass. The anger returns to his face and I know exactly where this is leading.

"Dad?" I say. "Do you think that's a good idea?"

He ignores me once more and gets into position behind the giraffe. He sets up where the neck meets the torso, spreading his legs and adjusting his grip. I watch as he raises the ax over his head, hesitating before coming down hard. I turn away just as he makes contact.

The sound is something I will never forget.

When I reopen my eyes he's in mid-swing, coming down for a second hack. This time I watch, both horrified and perplexed Dad can even go through with it.

Although the carcass looks days old and the flesh seems severely rotted, it takes Dad four swings to get all the way through it. When the neck finally detaches, it bounces on the ground like a decapitated serpent. Dad turns to me. He's covered in a splattering of Pollack art-style blood with a satisfied grin.

"How about that, eh?" he says.

I'm not sure if it's rhetorical or not. I don't have the slightest idea how to reply.

He moves over two feet along the neck and then starts

chopping again. I don't know if I can handle watching this all day.

"Dad, I—"

"It's fine. You go on. I can handle it from here," he says, as if he is reading my mind.

"Thanks. I'm going for a walk."

I go through the house and directly out the front door. I need air, fresh air. I walk down the street, heading to the one place I know will be quiet.

SIXTEEN
RICHARD

I need some better tools. This ax is like fifty years old. Well, not quite, but it seems like it. I have to put extra exertion into every swing just to make progress. I can feel my hands blistering already. This is going to be tough.

With Lacey gone I get even more focused, ignoring the pain and exhaustion. I know my time is limited and I have a ton to do. I finish the neck, cutting as close as I can to the bottom of the skull. The thing is huge. I consider splitting the head in two, but I'm worried about shattering it into unmanageable pieces. The body is so large I can't even comprehend cutting it up. Instead I move to the legs, severing each of them and then chopping those up at each joint. I have to keep reminding myself to keep it as clean as I can.

As I'm hacking away I can't help but think about Kara. Last night we spoke until I fell asleep. She told me everything. And even though it's much worse than I imagined, somehow having her there explaining it all to me made me feel better. My situation is far more fucked if even half of what she said comes true, but with her guidance I know we can get through this.

I asked Kara about bringing Lacey in on it, but she thought that was a bad idea. She thinks it will only frighten Lacey to hear her mother's voice coming from the urn. I agreed. When the time is right we can explain everything to her, but for now it's best we don't put any more stress on her than needs to be. She's dealing with enough as it is.

SEVENTEEN
LACEY

The sight of my dad hacking away at the rotten animal reminds me of how much I miss my mom. I ache for her. She would know what to do about the giraffe carcasses. She certainly wouldn't be hacking them up with an old ax.

When I get to the break in the neighborhood, where the city cemetery is, I sigh at the sight of Renee sitting on her bike with two other classmates. They stop talking when they see me and stare as if I was the subject of their conversation.

"Great," I mutter.

Joey and Luke smirk and I already know what's coming.

"There she is," Luke starts, "Daughter of the Psycho!"

Joey laughs like it's the funniest thing he's ever heard. He's always been Luke's best audience.

"Hey, guys," I reply as if I hadn't heard him, "just passing through." I put my head down and walk into the cemetery, hoping to god they don't follow me.

"Where you going?" Luke asks. "Visiting your mom?"

Joey bursts into another laughing fit. His gaggles sound like a mixture between a seasick rooster and a moaning cat in heat. I wonder how they can stand the sound of it.

"I don't think she's buried in there," Renee says, pedaling away from them. I can hear her tires grinding through the dirt as she comes up behind me.

"It was a joke!" Luke shouts.

I glance back and see the two boys walking in the other direction. I'm not sure I can deal with them today. Renee, on the other hand, whom seems determined to bug me every chance she gets, I realize I will have to deal with.

"I came here to be alone," I say as she pulls up beside me.

"I figured that," she replies but doesn't get the hint. "I bet your dad is making it impossible to be at home."

"Dad's fine. He's staying busy."

"Everyone's still talking about him."

"I can tell," I say.

"Oh, you mean Luke and Joey. We were just trying to figure out how he got the giraffes in your yard. Once is pretty impressive but two days in a row is ridiculous," she tells me.

"Almost too hard to believe, isn't it?" I realize they don't know the third is being chopped up as we speak. I hope it stays that way.

"Yeah, that's what I was telling them. Have you figured out how he did it?"

"He didn't do it. It's not possible, Renee. I've been with him. He's not the one doing it." I turn down a path to my left, quickly separating from her.

Renee turns through the grass, weaving between headstones in order to catch up.

"So what's your explanation?" she asks.

"I don't have one. Not yet anyway." I don't feel comfortable telling her what Ms. Plume said. I consider just leaving out the zombie apocalypse part and telling her the rest but quickly decide against saying anything.

"Alright," she says in a tone that makes me want to smack her. "I thought it might help talking about it, but if you really want to be alone . . ."

"I do."

"See ya," she says and turns around, pedaling back to the cemetery entrance.

Once the sound of her bicycle is out of range I can finally breathe. I search out a good sitting spot and make my way to it. It's a nook between two large roots under one of the larger trees in the cemetery. I sit on the grass and pull my knees up to my chest. I wonder if my life will ever be normal again. Maybe this is the new normal and I have to adjust. The thought feels crushingly heavy. My life is in ruins.

I close my eyes and lean my head back against the bark, not so much to nap, but more so to pull even further away from the world around me. It feels like I'm falling down an endless black well. Before I know it, my eyes are struggling to stay open.

I notice the grass bouncing, shifting up and down. At first I think it's concentrated to one spot, just beside a gravestone, but then I see other areas of grass doing the same. It dawns on me that the bouncing grass is only happening in areas next to graves.

I rub my eyes and try to blink out the obvious hallucination. It isn't working. The grass is bouncing harder and higher. The mound closest to me separates and I see black soil in the cracks. I put my hands to the ground, feeling a slight vibration, keeping my eyes locked on the cracking, bouncing mound.

I let out a tiny scream when five wiggling fingers sprout from the black soil. A whole hand follows after, grasping at the air for purchase.

Suddenly every mound, by every gravestone, cracks open and corpse hands shoot out.

This is it! This is what Ms. Plume told me would happen. This is what my mom warned her about. I can't believe my eyes, it's really happening. Zombies! A zombie uprising!

I jump to my feet, leaning my weight back against the tree. I'm terrified one will burst out from under me and pull me into the dirt.

Arms are followed by heads, followed by torsos and, finally, legs. I watch in horror, petrified in place, pinned against the tree with fear. They struggle to their feet, balancing on wobbly legs. There must be a couple hundred stumbling toward me, all in various states of decay. All of them frightening images straight out of my darkest nightmares.

I tell myself to run but my legs aren't listening, they're solid stone, frozen in place. I've never been this weak before. I always find the strength to pull through but, for some reason, this time I can't.

"Please," I plead with my body. "Just run!"

I start to shake uncontrollably as the closest zombie reaches me. His bone fingers clench onto my arms, digging into my skin.

I scream. It's all I can muster. Behind the first, several others close in, their jaws unhinged, leading teeth first. I shut my eyes and await the painful bites.

"Hey! Hey!"

My eyes shoot open. I'm sitting in the nook between the roots. There are no signs of zombies. No walking corpses or disturbed graves. It was all a dream. A dark, vicious dream.

"Hey!"

I look to my left and see a man walking on the path. I wave.

"The cemetery closes at dusk," he says.

It's the caretaker, I guess. "I'm leaving," I tell him and stand up.

"Are you okay?" he asks when I get near him. He's wearing dark coveralls and thick gloves. I can see dirt stains on his knees.

"Yep. Sorry, I just lost track of time."

"You haven't been messin' around with any of the sites, have you?"

"No, I just sat down and fell asleep."

"We've had a few vandals lately."

"Vandals?" I ask.

"Graverobbers."

I think about my dream and about what Ms. Plume said. I wonder if zombies are real and climbing out of their graves. "I haven't seen anything."

"Well, no more night visits. Alright?"

"Yeah, I didn't mean to, just fell asleep." I start walking backward, and then turn, quickening my pace to a fast walk. I head straight toward the cemetery entrance. I glance around at the headstones as I go, glad my mom isn't buried here. I don't think I'll ever be able to come back after a dream like that.

Behind me, the man continues walking in the other direction and I slow down a little. My eyes are darting from headstone to headstone. The fear from the dream is still very real. Once I finally get to the gates and step onto the street, I feel like I can breathe normally again. I try to laugh it off, but the decrepit, teeth-chattering zombie faces still flash in my mind. Their hollowed faces and white, lifeless eyes were staring at me with ravenous intentions and my body was refusing to run.

"Just a dream," I remind myself.

There's no sign of Luke or Joey, or Renee, for that matter. I would normally be relishing this time alone, but I'm still quivering from the dream.

I get home just as the last bit of sun disappears from the sky and full darkness envelopes the neighborhood. I walk up the driveway, staring at the empty lot next door. For some reason, Ms. Plume's car is parked in front of it. I get the feeling someone is watching me, hiding in the tall grass. I wonder if the old bat is wandering around in there, not realizing her house is two doors over. I consider checking, make sure she hasn't fallen down or something, but the whole situation is giving me the creeps. Instead, I go inside.

The house is dark and feels empty. I know that means Dad is already in bed, once more shutting himself away from the world and away from me.

I go straight to a back window and check the yard. I'm surprised to see him out there shoveling loose dirt into a hole. I run to the back door and step onto the porch.

"Dad?" I call out. "You're still out here?"

"Just about done," he replies.

I reach inside and flip on the light so he can see. It's hard to believe he stood out here all day, cutting up a giraffe and *burying* it.

He flings the last pile down and walks back to the shed, putting the shovel and the ax back in it. When he gets close I see how filthy he is. Equal amounts of dirt and blood cover his clothes. I can see he is worn out and exhausted. I know it's been a long time since he's worked a full day like that.

I want to say something to him. I want to thank him, but I stay silent while he walks by me. He goes inside and straight up the stairs and I know I'm not going to see him any more tonight.

I feel like we should be bonding. I feel like this is the time when we are supposed to come together and get past the grief like a family. Instead, it feels like we are further apart than ever. It feels like the last bit of whatever makes a family a family is disappearing. Soon we will just be two strangers living in the same house. The memory of our happy family will be completely lost to the point where we will barely even recognize each other.

I suddenly feel even more saddened by the idea of losing the memory of family than I do at the loss of my mother. She would be devastated if she knew her death was causing us to fall apart. She would grab both of us by the hand and physically bring us together, forcing us to get through this if she were still here. I can see her determined face, not stopping until Dad and I are hugging and sobbing, apologizing to one another.

I think maybe this realization is her trying to tell me not to give up. Maybe this is her way of reaching me and forcing me to make the first move. If Dad isn't willing to stand up for us, I'm going to have to do it.

I go up the stairs, focused and motivated like never before. I reach the top of the steps and turn to his door. It's opened just enough that I can see he isn't in bed. My mom's urn isn't there either. Beneath the bathroom door I can see light spilling out. I lean my head in and hear the shower on. My focus and motivation drop off instantly and a new form of rejection hits me. I know nothing has changed from one moment to the next, but I can't help but feel rejected.

I go to my room and lie down in bed. My stomach grumbles but I have no urge to do anything but sleep.

EIGHTEEN
RICHARD

I'm filthy. I'm tired. I have a newfound respect for men who dig holes. It may be the toughest job there is, arguably. I think about what Kara said to me. It seems ridiculous, but I trust her.

You trust a voice that sounds like her coming from an urn.

"It is her," I say as I turn on the shower, twisting the knob to make it hotter.

"It's who?" Kara asks.

I look back at the urn, sitting on the counter next to the bathroom sink. The mirror behind it is already starting to fog.

"No one, just mumbling," I reply.

I struggle to take my clothes off. My muscles are already feeling stiff. I nearly fall over while trying to remove my dirt-stained socks. Once I'm completely nude, I step into the steaming hot shower and quickly adjust the temperature so it's more bearable. As much as I want to burn off my skin, tainted with rotten giraffe flesh, I know I can't handle the pain.

I grab a bar of soap and start scrubbing. After a few minutes my mind drifts and I picture the giraffe lying in poorly segregated chunks just below the surface of my backyard. I wonder what the decomposition process will be like. I wonder how much time I really have.

NINETEEN
LACEY

I wake up to a sudden thumping on my door. "Are you up for some physical labor today?" Dad asks as he opens the door.

"What?"

"We need to dig another hole."

It takes me a second to process what he's saying. "You mean for a giraffe?" I ask, rubbing the sleep from my eyes.

"That's right," he says. "Get up and put on some old clothes and we'll run to the hardware store. I have to get a few things first."

"Dad?"

"Go on."

I want to protest for a multitude of reasons, mainly the fact that I'm not sure I can watch him cut up another giraffe, but realize our choices are limited. Maybe this is the only way. At least he seems to want to do it together.

The car ride is quiet. Dad isn't saying a thing, although he seems in a decent mood. I want to speak up and say we need to come together and spend more time together and get through this together but then realize we are sitting two feet from each other, alone in the car. We are together. It all sounds silly now in my head. I feel like a small child trying to tell an adult how things work. I decide to stay quiet.

At the hardware store I feel like everyone is staring at us. Our town isn't what I would consider a small town but I suppose small enough that the rumors of our situation have probably spread pretty quickly. I imagine half the town knows by now. I move my eyes to the floor to avoid making eye contact.

Dad stops at the lawn and garden section. I glance up at him just in time to see his shoulders shrug in that I-guess-this-is-what-I-need sort of way. The way a person does when they are pretending to know more than they do.

We return home with two new shovels, a wheelbarrow, and a chainsaw. I had no idea my dad even knew how to use a chainsaw. I'm still not sure.

It's early, mid-morning, and the neighborhood is quiet. All I can think about is him waking all the neighbors and seeing their horrified faces when they realize the noise is my dad chopping up a dead giraffe. I'm still wondering if there is a quieter, less intrusive way.

"Dad?"

He ignores me and points to a spot just beside the carcass. "We'll start digging there," he says. The spot is about ten feet from the hole he dug the night before.

I can tell he's in one of his zoned-out states, the kind where it's nearly impossible to reach him. He hands me one of the shovels and then takes the other and goes to the designated spot, kicking the spade down into the grass. I follow after him, mimicking his shoveling technique.

After the first hour we take a short break for water and a light lunch, and then we are right back at it. Digging a hole—a grave large enough to fit a giraffe in—is no easy task. Dad outlines the size we will need with stabs to the ground, creating a circle about the size of a child's pool.

When we get through the second hour we have the full diameter scooped out, though we've only gotten a little more than a foot in depth. My arms are achy and my hands are showing signs of blistering. It's been a long time since I've dug a hole, and even then it was nothing this size, nothing the size of a grave.

Dad seems possessed, not saying a word to me the entire time we've been out here. He's staring down, shoveling three times as fast as I am. I can tell his mind is moving even faster. I wonder where he's at mentally. I wonder if he would even notice if I left.

By the afternoon, the hole is close to five feet deep. I have to stand inside of it in order to get my shovel into the dirt. My arms are jelly. I feel like my muscles have given up on me, but I keep digging despite it. Dad climbs out of the grave and I watch him stab his shovel into the ground. He goes to the chainsaw and picks it up, examining it. Right away I get anxious. I know as soon as he starts it up the whole neighborhood will come running to see what the crazy man is up to. I'll never be able to live this down.

He fills it with gas from the small tank we use for the

lawnmower and then starts it up. Even in the hole it's louder than I thought it would be. I toss my shovel out and climb up, slipping back in twice before finally getting out. I move away from my dad and the giraffe, realizing it's going to be messy, and watch despite knowing I shouldn't.

Dad walks to the limbs-side of the giraffe and lifts the chainsaw up so he can get in close. He makes the first cut on the front right leg, chopping into it where it meets the body. There is no way to tell how long it's been dead, but this flesh seems easy to cut. Chunks and blood fling from the blades, kicked into the air a few feet before splattering on the fence and ground. He quickly gets through the first leg and then moves on to the next.

Shortly after getting all four legs removed, the smell of rot starts to hit me. When he cuts into the stomach the smell intensifies to the point I feel like I'm going to vomit. I gag and dry heave before lifting my sleeve up over my nose and moving away. I try my best to muffle it, breathing through my mouth, but the smell of rotten guts is too strong. I turn to my left and puke out the sandwich I had earlier.

Dad is clearly in some sort of whacked-out zone, as he seems to be having no issue at all with the scent of decayed giraffe. He's slicing through the thing's torso like it's something he's done a thousand times before. Once he's completed the body, Dad cuts up the neck into a half dozen pieces. When he finally turns the chainsaw off, both he and the majority of the surrounding yard are drenched in a dark, bloody flesh and viscera mix. He looks like he just dove into a pool of it.

"That ought to do it," he says, setting the chainsaw on the ground beside me.

I'm still battling the feeling of upchucking and get queasy just by the sight of him. All I can do is nod.

"Well, let's get to it," he says.

I watch as he walks back to the sliced up carcass and starts picking up pieces and tossing them into the hole. The first few chunks thud as they hit the soil, but everything after that sounds like a wet slap as they collide into other pieces. With each toss and drop, the scent of the rotten meat gets even stronger, becoming more airborne now that it's being moved about.

"Dad . . ." I try to let him know, but after the first word I'm once again vomiting.

He looks back at me and holds up his hand in a semi-wave. I guess he is letting me know he can handle the rest himself. After spitting out acidic bile lingering in my throat, I stumble back to the porch and sit on the steps. I take deep breaths into my sleeve and settle my stomach as much as I can.

When Dad gets the last of it in the hole he moves right away to the shovel and starts tossing the loose dirt on top of the chopped-up pieces. I feel bad that he's doing all the work but I know I won't be able to help until the smell is gone.

I notice movement by the fence but when I turn to look there isn't anything there. It's on the opposite side of Ms. Plume's yard, the vacant side. I think about the night before. Something is going on over there. I walk over and peek through the cracks of the wooden privacy fence, but I don't see anything. I stand on my tip-toes and can get just high enough to see near the center of the overgrown lot, but again there isn't anyone there.

Dad shovels the last of the loose dirt onto a now protruding pile. He stomps on top of it, trying to get it down a bit but there's just too much dirt left over.

"Not bad, eh?" he says, stepping off the pile.

"It looks like we have two enormous graves in the backyard," I reply.

He glances back at it and then to me and says, "Looks like a pile of dirt to me." He picks up the shovel I was using and then places both of them against the house. Then he picks up the chainsaw and gas tank and puts them in the shed.

On the way back to the house he pats me on the shoulder. "Thanks for helping. That went much quicker than last time."

"Dad, what if there's another one tomorrow?"

"Then we'll take care of it too."

"We can't spend every day digging holes and chopping up giraffes."

"We'll do what we have to."

TWENTY
RICHARD

For some reason, this is the best I've ever felt. I don't know if it's the physical labor or the late night conversations with Kara. Maybe a bit of both.

The last few months I felt like my life was stalling. Kara's illness and subsequent death brought the whole family to a standstill. I realize I was struggling to find a purpose to keep going. As weird as the giraffe situation has been, I think it's pulling me out of my depression. I think it's giving me a purpose to keep going.

I look over at Lacey. She reminds me of her mother more and more every day. I wish I could share the plan with her. I think it would help her find a purpose too.

TWENTY-ONE
LACEY

Dad goes inside and right up the stairs. I hope it's to shower the guts off. The stench is still lingering on him. I sit on the porch for a bit longer, watching the sun in its last leg of the day. I wonder how many more days will be like this one. I wonder if I am destined to spend my summer vacation digging holes in the backyard. The thought fills me with a new layer of dread.

"Eventually, you'll run out of yard," someone says.

My eyes dart to the fence by the vacant lot side, where I thought I had seen someone earlier, but there is still no sign of anyone.

"Over here."

I look to her side of the yard and see the top of Ms. Plume's tiny head breaching the fence.

"Oh, hey, Ms. Plume," I reply and walk over. "I guess you saw?"

"It was hard to miss with all that racket going on."

"Yeah, I told him it would be loud."

"Tell your father there isn't any point in burying them that deep. Soon the whole neighborhood will be covered in corpses. Keep the graves shallow."

I stand up tall, try and look her directly in the eye. It's hard to believe the things she is saying. It feels a little like she is pulling my leg. Like any minute a camera crew will come popping out of the bushes and tell me I'm on a reality television show and we will all laugh. I glance over my shoulders.

She taps on the fence with a bony knuckle that sounds like it's made of stone.

I look back at her. She seems gloomy.

"Tell your father not that deep. It's important—"

I cut her off, "Yes, I know. Soon the whole neighborhood will be covered."

"He's going to regret it when he needs them," she says and then walks away.

I stare at the spot she was occupying, my mind running through her words one by one, trying to find a hidden meaning. I'm coming up short.

"I think she's just crazy. Yep, I'm sure of it," I say out loud. *Need them.* I don't get it.

I decide to go inside and lose myself in the internet. I need some answers. As I'm going up the stairs, I begin to wonder if we are the only ones having these dead animal issues. I wonder if there are others out there having to deal with our same situation. Maybe instead of a giraffe, they are burying a hippopotamus carcass. I almost laugh out loud at the idea. Trying to deal with a hippo would be twenty times more comical and difficult.

I go in my room and sit at the desk, turning on my laptop. I feel silly googling giraffe carcasses so I just type in *random dead animal in backyard*. Thousands of hits come back. I try wording it a few different ways before finally specifying a giraffe carcass. There are numerous articles and blogs on giraffes and carcasses but nothing on someone finding one in their backyard. It feels hopeless. I slam the laptop shut in frustration.

I consider pulling up one of the social media sites I have accounts on and rarely use, but I can already picture the resulting comments and trolling mockery I will receive. Not to mention the last time I was on I kept getting hounded by older guys sending me PMs. I feel repulsed by the idea and decide against social media. I need real human interaction.

Calling Renee feels just as repulsive. I think about Tony, the cashier at the corner store, and remember how I came off a bit harsh last time I saw him. We've been dancing around each other for a while now. Maybe today is the day I make the first move. At least put us in a situation where we can have a conversation outside of the store and see where it goes from there? Although the idea of any type of romantic relationship is the last thing on my mind right now, I just want a conversation that doesn't involve my family's dysfunction.

I consider showering but decide to just wash my hands and face off instead. I redo my ponytail and change into clean jeans and my black hoodie. I'm out the door before Dad notices and feel slightly guilty for not saying something or leaving a note. It was a nice change of pace spending the majority of the day with him, even if it was spent silently digging a hole before watching him hack up a dead animal.

I walk the street, looking up at the recently arrived night sky. The stars feel brighter tonight. I look from one to another until it feels like I'm being crushed by the overwhelming amount of world out there I've never set a foot into and probably never will.

I'm happy to see Renee's house is dark. The family car is gone. Probably out to dinner at a nice restaurant. I picture her and her nosy-ass mom shoveling food into their gaping mouths. I picture her dad and her little brother slopping down chicken wings with greasy fingers. When we were younger I stayed the night at her house a few times. Her parents' obesity always grossed me out, but I never said anything to her. Even back then I could tell she was sensitive about it. Now I know it's a sore spot, especially since she's put on a few pounds herself.

My stomach starts growling again. There's still another mile to the corner store. I try and take my mind off it, but the only other place it goes is the giraffe. I smile. The two things on my mind are Renee's fat ass, shitty family and a dead giraffe, and my stomach is still grumbling despite it. I suppose vomiting up my lunch didn't help anything.

I struggle through the last mile but finally arrive at the corner store. There is one car at the gas pump but otherwise it appears empty. I walk in and my eyes go right to the register. I'm expecting the normal routine interaction that Tony and I usually have, but he isn't there.

"Welcome," says an older woman with silver hair and a ladybug body. She squints through thick-lensed glasses.

I nod and continue to the back of the store. Where's Tony? He's always here. I wonder if something terrible happened. I wonder if he died.

I pace the aisles, not even paying attention to the products. I realize I probably look like I'm casing the place and stop at a section of bagged seeds and nuts. I grab some shelled sunflower seeds and a bag of mixed nuts and move to the refrigerated drinks. I find a bottle of water and take everything to the front counter.

"That it?" the ladybug says.

"Yes." I dig into my pocket and pull out a wad of crumpled bills. I consider asking about Tony but decide against it. I don't want to seem too eager, in case it gets back to him somehow. When the transaction is complete I go back outside, uncapping the bottle of water right away.

"Warm night," someone says. I turn to my left where Tony leans against the wall.

"Uh, yeah," I reply, taking a swig of the water. "I was wondering what happened to you. For a second there I thought maybe you transformed into somebody's grandmother." He gives me a confused look until I point to the cashier inside.

"Oh, right. Nah, we just switched shifts today. I covered her day shift so she's doing my night," he says. "Happens sometimes."

"Then why are you still hanging around?"

"My ride is late. Like always." He shifts his weight from one leg to the other before putting his hands in his pockets.

"That sucks." I hold up the bag of seeds. "Sunflower seed?"

He smirks. "I'm okay. Thanks, though."

I stare at him for what feels like too long. Damn, I'm terrible at this kind of stuff. I want to say something but nothing else comes to mind. Instead I start to walk home.

"Hey, wait up." Tony comes running up beside me. "You don't have to run off."

"Sorry, I'm just gonna go home."

"I can walk with you. If that's okay," he says.

"What about your ride?"

"I've been standing there for an hour. I have a feeling they forgot about me."

"I know the feeling."

TWENTY-TWO
RICHARD

I take Kara into the bathroom with me and set her on the floor while I undress. My clothes are saturated with blood. I should probably just throw them out. I turn on the shower and then pick up the urn. We used to love to shower together. It wasn't even the sex, just holding each other in the warm water was all we needed.

"I miss you more each day," I say as I close the curtain behind us. The water tings off the urn, bouncing in my eyes.

"You don't have to miss me. I'm here whenever you need me."

"You know what I mean. I want to hold you."

"You are holding me," she says.

I close my eyes and lean into the urn, kissing it softly. I feel her kissing me back and I can't help but get turned on. Within seconds I am hard and stroking myself.

"It's been a while," Kara says. "I was wondering when you were going to make love to me again."

I open my eyes and lift my lips off the urn, then unscrew the top. I place it on the ledge and then move it down to my waist. The water starts to fill it before I can turn away from the showerhead. I look inside and see the ashes are soupy and muddy.

"Sorry," I mutter.

"Don't be. I'm ready. I want it," she says.

I drop the urn down to my waist again and move my cock inside it. I slide into the muddied ashes, pushing in as far as I can go before I bump into the bottom. She feels so warm and soft. I nearly orgasm right away. Slowly I start pumping my hips, holding the urn steady as I thrust. Kara moans and it prompts me to increase my speed.

"I can't believe I'm making love to you again," I say, panting between breaths.

"Fuck me. Harder! Harder!"

I push the urn against the back wall of the shower and go at it as hard and fast as I can. After a minute I can't contain it any longer and explode into the urn. My cum mixes in with the muddy ashes as I shudder the last few seconds of the orgasm.

When I pull out, I make sure I get as much of the ash off my penis as I can. The rest I wash off and watch as it swirls down the drain. I place the cap back on the urn and set it on the ledge while I finish cleaning off.

TWENTY-THREE
LACEY

I crunch on sunflower seeds as we walk along the dark road. I keep looking over at Tony to make sure he's really there, walking me home. Something feels surreal about the entire thing. I almost want to reach over and touch his arm, just to make sure this is really happening.

"What?" he asks when he catches me staring.

"Nothing." I look down at the pavement.

"I heard about your mom dying. I wanted to say something last time I saw you but it felt forced and weird. I'm sure you're tired of hearing people say sorry to you all the time," Tony says.

"You have no idea." I chuckle. "Like they think that will help comfort me in any kind of way."

"I always wondered why people said that."

"I guess out of habit more than anything. Either that or they don't really know what else to say," I tell him.

We both fall silent for several steps until I toss another handful of seeds into my mouth.

"What happened to your hands?" he asks suddenly.

I glance down at my palms and remember the blisters. "Just some yard work injuries." I hold my hand up to him so he can get a better look. "You should see what the shovel looks like."

"I think you should take a break from gardening." He touches my hands gently while he examines them.

I'm glad the rumors of the giraffe fiasco haven't reached him yet. I'm sure the story will make its way around to the corner store sooner or later, but for the moment he seems oblivious and I'm happy about that.

I pull my hand away. "I wish I could."

"Your dad making you do it?" he asks.

"Not really. Look, we can talk about something else. I don't want this walk to be about my family. It's not something I like to talk about."

He puts his hands up in a surrendering gesture. "Sure, I understand. We can talk about whatever you want."

"I want to know about you, Tony the cashier." As I say it, I realize that's really all I know about him. I wonder if walking home in the dark with him is the best decision.

"Not much to me," he replies. "I'll be a senior next year. Hopefully getting into State. Hope to make the football team."

I meet his eyes and we both laugh.

He starts again, and this time I can hear the solemnity in his voice. "Yeah, I dropped out of school last year. I'll probably be working at the corner store for the rest of my life."

"No car?"

"I failed the written test last year and haven't tried again yet. You?"

"I've got my learner's permit but I haven't been practicing much," I tell him.

"Glad to see I'm not the only one procrastinating." He kicks a rock across the road. "Something about this town makes me want to just give up. I used to have ambition. At least, I thought I did. I can't even remember what it feels like."

We walk silently for a few more steps. I get the urge to vent all my issues but realize I actually like this guy. Telling him how miserable and fucked up my life is is probably not the best way to keep him around. Instead, I pop another handful of sunflower seeds into my mouth.

"Damn, that must've been painful!" he blurts out.

"Excuse me?" I mumble through my seed-filled mouth.

He points across the road to what initially appears to be a dark mound. "Cat, I think." He moves closer, crossing the double yellow lines, and leans in for a better look. "Yeah, definitely was a cat. Not so much anymore."

I swallow and cross the street, moving next to him. The dark mound transforms into a decimated pile of twisted and crushed cat hair, bones, blood. I can see its stomach popped, spilling intestines out around its waist. The skull is flat and what I can only guess is cat brains are still leaking out from a large crack running down the middle of its head.

I turn away. All I can think about is the rotten giraffe carcasses.

"You okay?" he asks.

I walk to the other side of the street, getting as far from the roadkill cat as I can. "Yeah, I've just had my fill of dead things."

"I didn't even think about that. Sorry." He walks up next to me. "Shit! I said sorry, just like everyone else does. I'm fucking this up, aren't I?"

"What? No." I start to walk. "Let's just get away from it."

Tony follows but I can tell he's upset with himself. He stays a step behind. Once we're far enough away that the stink of a dead animal is no longer harassing my nostrils, I slow down for him.

"Hey," I say as he catches up.

"Hey."

"I know I'm kind of a mess right now. I do like you but things are so crazy right now," I tell him.

"I fucked up. Things were going alright before the dead cat thing. I knew I should've left it alone."

"No. It's not that. You didn't fuck anything up." We start walking again. I can see my house in the distance. The lights are all off. Dad probably didn't even check to see if I was there. "I'm the one who's messing it up. I'm dealing with a lot. It's not you."

"Oh, 'the it's-not-you, it's-me' thing. Got it."

"No, I didn't mean it that way."

"It's all good. I was just walking you home anyway. Don't get too full of yourself." Tony walks ahead of me, speeding up.

"Where are you going?" I call out.

"Home. I live a few streets over."

My heart drops. He lives in my neighborhood. All this time, I had no idea. I realize this also means he must know about the giraffes. I wonder if he was playing dumb or, if by some crazy miracle, he hasn't heard yet. The gossip will reach his house soon enough.

We walk, an increasing amount of space growing between us. He passes my house first and keeps going. When I finally reach it, I stop at the edge of the yard and look at the dark, lonely house, before turning to Tony. "Thanks for the walk!" I shout to his back.

He raises a hand in the air as if he's waving me off. He doesn't turn around.

I start toward the side door but decide to check the backyard first. I open the gate and slip in. The yard is giraffe-free for the moment but it's early. I wander over to the dirt mounds, careful not to step directly on one. It's hard not to imagine the chopped up, rotten chunks of each giraffe just a few feet below the soil. I look around the rest of the yard, wondering how long the giraffe carcasses will continue to show up. I wonder if we have enough space for them.

A scratching sound comes from behind me. I glance toward the fence, to the empty lot beside us. I think I see movement between the cracks again, but realize it's the shadow of clouds as they start covering the moon. I hear soft thunder claps in the distance. I can smell the faintest hint of rain.

I move slowly to the fence, keeping my arms up near my head, just in case something horrific jumps out at me. When I reach it I don't see anything. I don't hear any more scratching sounds. Then the first few drops of rain thump down on the top of my head. It feels like the world might collapse and crush me to smithereens. Right now, I don't think I would mind being crushed to smithereens.

TWENTY-FOUR
RICHARD

"Kara?" I ask.

"What's wrong?"

I dry off the urn with one of the towels we stole from our last beach vacation. It was the last trip we took before the sickness began. Then I place her softly on the bed, pulling the comforter down and leaning her against the pillow. I go around the other side and lie down next to her. "I don't know if I have the strength to go back to work. I'm supposed to be in the office tomorrow. Between the hospital visits and taking the last week off, I don't have any more time left. I suppose Bill would let me have a few more days but it'd be without pay." Before she can respond I start again. "I just don't know how to go on."

"You can't go back to work. Who will take care of the giraffes? Lacey needs you here. You have to stick to the plan. In a few more days none of that stuff will matter anyway. Trust me," she says.

I lean in and cuddle next to her, spooning the urn. "I trust you."

TWENTY-FIVE
LACEY

I wake up to rain tapping the window. It must've stormed all night. I realize last night was the best sleep I've had in a while as I stretch across the bed. I sit up, taking note of the dim light outside. An overcast, rainy day. I go to the window and peek outside. There's another giraffe carcass. Of course there is. This is the first time I'm not surprised or alarmed in any way. It's become part of the morning routine now.

I get dressed in old jeans, a sweater, and thick socks. Despite it being midsummer, I feel a chill all the way to my bones.

As I'm brushing my teeth I hear Dad stirring in his room. I can hear his muffled voice. I have a strong feeling he isn't talking on the phone. I try not to let it bother me.

When I get downstairs, I go straight for the coffee. I make enough for both us. Then I dig through the cabinets, wondering why I didn't think to pick up something for breakfast when I was at the corner store. That makes me think of Tony. I wonder if it's a lost cause between us now. I wonder if I should say anything to him or just leave it alone. I don't know if I can go back to the store.

Dad comes downstairs. He's holding Mom's urn.

"Hey," I say.

"Good morning," he replies, setting the urn down on the table near the back window. He shifts the curtains to the side and pulls up the blinds.

"Coffee?" I lift my mug to my mouth and take a slow sip.

"Yes, thanks. We've got another big day ahead of us." He adjusts the urn.

I set my mug down and grab one out of the cabinet for him. "Do you think it will ever end? I think we'll run out of yard to bury them soon." I pour his coffee and stir in some sugar. Then take it over to the table where he sits next to Mom's urn.

"I think it'll end when we get enough. Don't worry. As long as we get them in the ground every day we'll be okay." He slips his hand around the coffee mug. "Thanks."

"What do you mean enough? Enough for what?"

Dad goes quiet while he drinks his coffee. When he sets it back down I'm expecting an answer but instead he gets up and goes to put his boots on.

"Dad? Enough for what?"

"You'll see. Don't worry about it," he says. "We've got work to do. Get your boots and raincoat on. It looks like a wet one." He grabs his coat and goes outside.

I watch as he goes out to the shed, leaving me and Mom's urn in the kitchen. I look over at it, terrified my mom's ghost is in there. If she comes out and starts talking to me I'm making a run for it. Instead, it just sits there silently.

I get my boots and raincoat on and go outside. I set my coffee on the back porch, taking one more swig before putting gloves on. The stench from the rotten carcass seems intensified by the rain. I can see where the hard drops are bouncing off the old flesh. Blood is spreading out, turning the grass around it a strange shade of red.

I walk over to the spot where Dad stabbed the shovels into the ground. I'm assuming that's the next grave location. I grab the handle, already feeling the discomfort as the pressure of gripping it aggravates the blisters from the previous day. I wince through the pain and kick the spade into the dirt just as Dad starts up the chainsaw. I can't help but glance around the fence line, embarrassed by how loud the thing is, waiting for neighbors to pop their heads over and see what's going on. I try my best to ignore it and the neighbors.

After the first hour things are looking on schedule, despite the storm. The ground is saturated from the overnight rain and the digging is the easiest it's been since I've been doing it. I think about what Ms. Plume said and wonder if I should tell Dad we should leave the grave shallow. There's a small puddle forming in the bottom, making the shovel splash every time I strike down. It's soaking my jeans up to the knee and my socks are getting wet through my boots. I set the shovel down and go for a coffee break.

"Dad? Do you need anything?"

He ignores me and keeps chopping. His entire body is covered in both mud and blood. It drips down his face and limbs in dark brownish-red streaks. I look at his drenched hands and can't figure out how he can even hang on to the chainsaw in this mess.

I step onto the porch and see Mom's urn through the window. It's like she's watching over us as we work. For some reason the thought of that is comforting. I think I'm closer to insane than sane.

I grab my coffee. It's already cold. I consider going inside and making a fresh pot but I don't particularly want to be alone with the urn. I drink some of the cold coffee, turning my back to the window. It feels like eyes are on me, like Mom is watching, specifically. I finish off the rest of the mug and set it back on the railing. As I step off the porch and head back to the gravesite, something up above me catches my eye.

I squint into the cloudy sky. Raindrops fall into my face so I shield them with a hand. At first it looks like swirling dots of black, but the longer I stare the more I can see what appears to be a committee of circling vultures. They're high in the sky, but definitely staying right above our yard. I wonder how much longer we have until they decide to drop in and give us a visit. I pick up the shovel and continue digging, glancing up at the vultures every few minutes.

When Dad finishes cutting up the carcass, he cleans up the chainsaw and puts it away in the shed. I watch as he brings the pieces and chunks of giraffe over to the hole. He drops the head and it lands in a way that its face is right in front of me. I look into its one remaining eye. It reminds me of the time I went to the zoo and fed the giraffes. The big eyes and drooping lashes followed the lettuce I had in my hands. I look at the gnarled face and see the purple tongue hanging past exposed teeth, remembering the way the zoo giraffe pulled the lettuce from my hand.

I'm about two feet down and have the entire perimeter dug out when Dad joins me. He digs like a madman, kicking and scooping the shovel in twice as fast as I do. I watch him as I dig, it's almost like he thinks he's being observed. Then I remember Mom's urn in the window. He thinks she's watching him. He's showing off for her.

"Dad, maybe we shouldn't go so deep? It'll save time and energy, at least."

He ignores me.

After a few minutes I feel like I'm in his way more than helping, so I climb out. Dad doesn't even raise an eye. He's shoveling faster, making his way around the grave, tossing dirt in every direction. I back away, dodging flying soil, and trip on a giraffe leg. I fall to my ass, slipping all the way down so I'm lying in the yard. I look up at the circling vultures through the falling rain. I swear it looks like they are getting closer, but I can't be sure.

I look to my left and see Ms. Plume. She's just a sliver of a head, peeking above the fence. I raise my hand and wave to her. She does the same before briskly walking away and ducking back into her house. If it was anyone else I would be worried about the police being called but I know Ms. Plume won't tell anyone.

I sit up and look at the dirt and mud, the bones and rotten flesh covering our yard. It's almost becoming a normal sight. I push myself off the ground and stand just as Dad climbs up.

"I think that'll do it."

I glance into the hole. It's significantly shallower than the previous ones. "Are you sure?"

"Yep. Let's start filling it. Can you hand me those larger leg pieces behind you?" He points as he says it.

I lean down and grab one. The smell hits me like a solid object knocking into my face and I drop it back to the ground. "I don't know." I turn my head and let out a deep breath before inhaling mostly fresh air. Then I go back for the leg. As I lift it higher I feel the rainwater, blood, and flesh juices running off it and down my sweater sleeve. I quickly turn and hand it to Dad before flapping my arms and flinging off as much of the juices as I can.

One by one I grab the rotten pieces of giraffe and hand them to him. I have to take deep breaths between each handful, like I'm diving under the water each time I bend down. When we finish I feel strangely proud of myself for helping. Last time I couldn't even stand next to the chopped up pieces without throwing up.

Dad hands me a shovel and we start to fill in the grave. It's all mostly mud by now, adding weight to each scoop, but we quickly get through it. By the time we finish, I realize it's before lunch, and the fastest we've ever done this. As long as we can keep this up, maybe we will be alright.

TWENTY-SIX
RICHARD

I pat down the last of the dirt on the latest grave and take Lacey's shovel. I'm glad she stuck around this time, although she is still looking at me like I'm a stranger. Maybe I'm giving her the same look. I try to smile at her but it feels forced, so I quickly turn and take the shovels back to the shed. When I come back out she's standing on the porch waiting for me. I wish I could tell her more. I wish I had something comforting to tell her.

I walk by Lacey and go inside. I smile at Kara as I make my way to the sink, washing my hands and face. I'm glad she got to see me work today. I pick her up off the table and start upstairs.

"Where are you going?" Lacey asks.

"Just a quick shower."

"Want to maybe get some lunch together after?"

I hesitate, standing in the doorway, holding Kara close to me. "We'll see."

I hear my phone ringing upstairs. I don't even remember the last time I used it. I force another smile at Lacey and then turn to the steps.

Upstairs I see my phone sitting on the nightstand. I pick it up and read Terry's name on the screen. I swipe the answer button.

"Hello," I muster through a suddenly tightening throat.

"Hey, Rich," he replies. "It's almost noon and I haven't heard from you today. Just wanted to give you a call and see how things are going. You do remember today was your day to be back in the office?"

"Yes, I remember. I should've called. The morning kind of got away from me." I set Kara's urn down on the bed, leaning back against her pillow.

"It's understandable. Should I expect you this afternoon or do you need another day?" Terry asks.

I realize how great a boss he's been through all of this. I don't want to disappoint him.

I guess Kara sees the struggle on my face. She says, "You know you can't. In a few days there won't be any jobs for anyone to go to. You should end this now."

"Rich? You still there?" Terry asks.

"Yeah. Yeah. I'm uh, I'm sorry, Terry. I won't be coming back in."

"So tomorrow then?"

"No. Not tomorrow either. I'm not coming back in at all. I have to quit."

"What are you talking about? You've worked here for twelve years. I know this is a tough time for you but don't make any rash decisions."

"Terry."

"Look, take another week. It sounds like you need it. Hell, I'll even pay you for it. You take care of yourself and that kid of yours. Your wife would want that. Take care, okay? I'll call you in a few days."

"Terry."

The phone clicks and I realize he hung up before I could reply. I set it down on the nightstand, noting that it only has thirteen percent of the battery left. I should charge it, but it feels like there's no point. Instead I go to the bathroom and turn on the faucet. I take off my clothes, leave them in the increasing pile of blood and dirt-stained things that sit in the corner.

"You're not planning on leaving me out here are you?" Kara asks from the bed.

I look back to the urn and smile. "Wouldn't dream of it." I go back and scoop her up, carrying her across the room like I used to do when she was still alive. Together we get into the shower and make love again.

TWENTY-SEVEN
LACEY

I finish my shower before Dad and go downstairs to wait for him. It feels like we are slowly making progress. I hope he decides to go to lunch with me. I sit on the couch and watch the rain fall out front. I'm not sitting there long when a dark blur streaks by the window.

"What the hell?" I jump up and go look, scanning the front yard. I don't see anything in the grass, but as I make my way across to the driveway, I spot a black object lying on the car hood.

From the front window it's difficult to make out what it is, so I go around to the side door that leads directly to the driveway. As soon as I open the door, I can tell what the black object is: a vulture. Well, to be more specific, a dead vulture. I can see the wings spread out, the left wing cocked at an angle that makes it appear almost certainly broken. The feathers are ruffled, a few lying on the car and in the driveway. I can tell it's dead, even from the doorway. The thing's naked head is nearly severed, hanging on by a thin line of flesh.

I lift up my hood and step outside, walking down the steps and over to the car. There's a little bit of blood where the neck is snapped and hanging, but not nearly enough to make me believe it happened on impact. When I move around to the side and check out its face, I see dark, rotten flesh. It's bubbling around the eyes. It takes me a second to realize the bubbling is maggots, pulsing under the flesh, eating their way out.

I watch as the vulture's eye pops out, dangling by veins, followed by dozens of fat, little maggots. I jump back as they spread out all over Dad's car hood, writhing in the rainwater.

I look up into the sky and spot the committee, still circling high above our house. None of the other vultures seem bothered by their fallen companion. Before putting too much thought into how the bird fell or why it looks like it died long before the fall, I go back in the house and grab a plastic bag. When I return there are even more maggots crawling free and wriggling across the tiny puddles on the car's hood. I push my hand into the plastic bag and use it as a makeshift glove, then grab the vulture by the legs. I lift it off the car and take it straight to the trash can, dropping it inside. I go back to the car and swipe as many maggots off the hood as I can reach without soaking my sleeves in the rainwater, then I go back to the trash can and drop the plastic bag inside.

"What are you doing?" I hear Dad say from the open side door.

"There was a dead bird on the car. I threw it in the trash

can."

He looks over at the car and then back to me. "I think I'll take you up on that lunch offer," he says. "Just let me grab the keys and I'll be right out."

I nod, unable to hide the excited smile that starts to spread across my face.

When Dad comes back out, he's holding his keys in one hand and Mom's urn in the other. My excitement fades. I thought his acceptance of lunch together was going to be a sign of us making progress. I thought maybe he was beginning to get better, but after bringing the urn downstairs this morning and now bringing it along with us to lunch, I think maybe things are worse than ever.

I open the door to the front passenger seat, but I'm met with a strange look from Dad.

"I think your mother would like to sit up front with me," he says. "Why don't you grab one of the seats in the back, okay, Boo?"

I watch as he sits down and sets the urn in the passenger seat, pulling the seatbelt across it and strapping it in. I sit in the backseat behind the urn. I want to say something, to tell him how crazy he's being, but I hold my tongue.

Dad starts the car and we back out the driveway. When he shifts to drive, I see Renee sitting on her bike. She's right next to the car. Her eyes aren't on me or my dad, they're locked onto the urn. I can see her expression, it's changing in slow motion, going from curious to freaked-the-fuck-out. At the last second she mouths 'The fuck', just as she spots me in the backseat. Before I can mouth any words in reply, Dad is driving us away.

I drop my face into my palms.

Just as I thought things might be turning out okay, this happens. I know everyone in town will hear about this, including Tony, before we even get back home.

We drive silently at first, my mind racing with dread, hearing all the comments and gossip that is probably already spreading. It gets so loud I put my hands over my ears. "Dad, can we put on some music?"

The past several months we've only driven in silence, both of us lost in our heads, thinking about the sickness that was taking, and ultimately took, Mom. I'm not sure what he will say.

He looks over at the urn and says, "What do you think, honey? '80s?"

I sit quietly, hoping the urn will speak. As crazy as that sounds, I'd prefer to find out that somehow her spirit is sitting in there and able to communicate with us, rather than the alternative.

I don't hear anything. Not even a peep.

Dad nods his head, as if she spoke to him and he is in agreement. "Okay!" he says. Then he turns on the radio, changing the stations until he sets it on the oldies '80s station. The car fills with electronic pop, George Michael singing lyrics so obnoxious I can't help but smile. I'm filled with equal parts nostalgia and dread. I have a feeling I will end up in the loony bin with '80s new wave hits repeating in my mind for the rest of my life.

A few minutes later we stop at a local restaurant. It's one we used to frequent before Mom got sick. Dad puts the car in park and kills the ignition. He takes off his seatbelt and then unbuckles the urn, picking it up. He's taking it inside with us.

He looks back at me and smiles. "I can't remember the last time we all went out like this."

"Dad, I—" I start but he's already out of his seat and shutting the car door. "This can't be happening."

I follow him inside. We're led to a booth. There's only a handful of people in the place but they are all staring at us, at Mom's urn cradled in Dad's hands. I look down at the table. I can feel my face flushing red. I quickly order a water and try not to sigh when Dad orders an iced tea for Mom. The waitress doesn't even bat an eye. I can't imagine how weird it must get in here if this isn't the strangest thing she's seen.

We sit in silence. I watch Dad caress the side of the urn and feel vomit creep up my throat. He's staring at it like it's Mom. It's like he discovered her all over again. He looks like a teenager in love.

I try not to make eye contact with anyone else in the restaurant. Throughout the meal, I feel them watching me. I know what they're thinking. I'm thinking the same thing. When we finally finish eating—well, Dad and I finish, the plate in front of the urn is sitting untouched—I nearly run out of the restaurant.

The rain has become a light mist. I stand in it, finally able to breathe normally. When Dad comes out he goes right to the car, putting Mom in the passenger seat again. I wait until they're both buckled and the car is on before I get in.

TWENTY-EIGHT
RICHARD

"Enjoying the rain?" I ask Lacey.

"Are you talking to me or Mom's urn?" she snaps back.

"You." I put the car in drive and pull out of the parking lot.

"It's nice."

I look over to Kara. When I look at her I no longer see the urn, I see my wife. I know that must seem strange to everyone, especially my daughter, but it is what it is. Whenever Lacey refers to her as the urn I feel a slight tick in my head. It's a different kind of anger. I'm not used to it. The past several months were filled with a hopeless kind of anger. This is the rage kind.

Kara meets my eyes and I swallow the rage back down. I shouldn't be angry right now. I should be happy. My wife is back.

The drive home is uneventful. Lacey is staring out the window. She's going through some kind of teenage angst.

Whenever she gets like this I find it's best just to give her space. She needs to learn pouting won't get her through life. Kara sits silently, bobbing her head to the music.

When we get home, the rain has completely stopped. Before I can even put the car fully into park, Lacey is out and running in the house. When I get out I see her friend Renee and a couple of boys riding bicycles in front of the house. I wave.

"That was really nice," Kara says as I pick her up. "But we have a lot of work to do."

"Yeah?" I'm not sure what she's referring to.

"You need to get that dead bird out of the garbage. We need to clean the bones. If the birds are starting to die, it won't be long now," she says. "Every bone has its place. We will need them all."

I set her on the steps and lift up the trash can's lid. I see the bird lying on top of a plastic bag. It looks twisted and rotten. There are maggots all over it. "Do I need to dig another grave?"

"No, we don't have time for that. It's starting quicker than I thought."

I pick up the bird by one of its wings. It stretches out, expanding nearly two feet as I raise it up out of the garbage. Maggots fall out of its head and chest like I'm picking up a busted pinata.

"Take it to the backyard," Kara says. "I'll explain how to clean the feathers and gristle."

I do what she says, plucking gray feathers and tearing scrawny meat from the hollow bones of the vulture. It takes longer than I expect it to, but by sunset I have a clean pile of bones. I leave them in the shed and head back to the house. When I get to the gate I see a cop car sitting in the driveway.

"Shit," I say. "Not that guy again."

"Who is it?" Kara asks.

"The deputy. I'll take care of it."

I walk around to the front of the house and see Lacey sitting on the front steps with Deputy Thompson. He looks at her with concern. "Deputy!" I announce as I approach.

He stands up and comes over, meeting me on the sidewalk before I can get close to Lacey.

"Nice to see you," I say, reaching out for a handshake.

He pauses, leaving me hanging.

"Is that your wife's urn?"

"Oh." I look down at Kara. "Yes."

"We've been getting calls about you acting strangely," Deputy Thompson says. "The neighbors are concerned."

"I don't see how carrying around my recently deceased wife is harmful to the neighbors. I'd like to think they'd mind their own business."

"Uh huh," he nods, crossing his arms. "And what about the dead animals?"

I glance at Lacey. I wonder if she's the one who alerted the police. "Just cleaning up the yard. Nothing out of the ordinary."

"Right," Deputy Thompson replies. "Where were you this afternoon? I checked around back, saw the dirt piles, but I didn't see you."

"I was in the shed."

"Doing what?"

"Look," I say and walk around him. I go to the front steps and sit down next to Lacey. "We're okay. We had a few more incidents with dead animals, a bird was on my car this morning, but we disposed of them properly. Nothing to worry about and no need to alert the police."

Deputy Thompson stands in front of us both. "Is that right?" He looks from me to Lacey and then back to me again.

"Yes," Lacey says.

"Yes, sir," I reply. "Sorry to waste your time."

"I'm going to continue swinging by here every few days. I don't want to see any more dead animals or get any goddamn calls from the neighbors about weird shit going on over here. You got it?"

"Got it," I say with a smile.

Lacey nods. Her eyes dart to the street. She's eyeing the kids on the bicycles.

Deputy Thompson turns and goes back to his car. As he's backing out the driveway he stops and says something to the kids.

"You think they're the ones that called us in?" I ask Lacey.

"Absolutely."

TWENTY-NINE
LACEY

I watch Deputy Thompson drive away. Renee, Joey, and Luke
sit on their bikes just past our house. I can hear them talking but
I can't tell what they're saying. I try and concentrate on their
voices but it's all too muffled and sounds like gibberish.

"Why do you think your friends called the police on us?" Dad
asks.

"They're not my friends."

"Oh, I thought that little girl was your friend. What was her
name again?"

"Renee."

"Right, Renee. She used to come by all the time," he says.
Then he looks down at the urn like he hears it saying something.
"Your mom says that you two had a fight or something."

"Dad, please. I don't like it when you talk to the urn. Mom's
dead." I get up and go in the house. I can't handle sitting there

while Renee and those goons laugh at us.

I go upstairs and straight to my room. I need some alone time. As nice as it is to have Dad around and participating in life again, it's equally dreadful knowing he's lost his mind. I don't know which version of him I prefer.

I lie on my bed and picture Dad out there with the urn, referring to it like it's Mom. I really think he sees her physical body instead of the urn. I imagine them continuing to have conversations and eating meals together. I wonder if he will start dressing the urn up in clothes and jewelry. I can see him taking her to all my school events and making me take family photos with it. I wonder how long it can go on before Deputy Thompson locks him up.

The officer seemed pretty convinced Dad is putting the dead animals in the yard on purpose. If he sees another giraffe in the backyard I'm sure he will, at least, take Dad in for questioning. I can't let that happen. I don't want to see my dad in the psych ward, or worse yet, in jail. Losing one parent is enough. We have to keep the giraffe carcasses hidden. Especially from Renee's peeping eyes.

I get up and go to the window. Slowly I push the blinds open just enough to get a good look outside. Renee and the boys are gone. I wonder what kind of stuff they were saying about me and Dad. I wonder what she's planning next.

Before I walk away, I see my dad moving around the front yard. He's still holding the urn as he goes over to what looks like another dead bird. I watch as he picks it up by the legs. I can clearly see it now. It's another vulture. He takes it around to the backyard, but doesn't see as another falls in the front.

"Shit, I have to get that up before Renee sees," I say to myself. I run out of the room and down the stairs. When I get outside I'm nearly knocked in the head by another dead vulture. When it bounces off the lawn, I see maggots sprinkle out. A handful of them fly in my direction and I have to turn my back to keep from getting slapped in the face by the things.

I quickly scan the road to make sure there is no sign of Renee and grab the two vultures up and run to the backyard. I fling them over the fence, unable to open the latch with both hands full of dead bird. I go to open the gate when I spot another falling bird.

It appears the vultures are slowly falling one by one.

When they are flying around above the house they appear to be alive and well, but as they hit the yard, they are not only dead, but look days' rotten.

"Damn."

I run back around the front and grab up the latest vulture, tossing it into the backyard just as another hits. This is quickly becoming an endless cycle. I check the sky again and try to get a count. There are at least seven more still circling.

Within the next five minutes, the rest of the vultures fall. Each one is just as dead and rotten as the previous. I scoop them up as they hit, dodging the maggots that get flung off on contact.

When the last of them has fallen and is tossed in the backyard, I finally go through the gate. It looks like a war zone. I've never seen so many dead birds in one spot. Feathers and blood pools, maggots and putrid, old flesh lie in pieces around the carnage.

I look around for Dad but I don't spot him anywhere. There's no way he could've gone inside without seeing the pile of dead birds. I scan the yard for somewhere to bury them, the giraffe carcasses take up so much room we will be out of space soon. When I settle on a spot, I go to the shed to get the shovel.

I open the door and see Dad inside, carving the flesh from a vulture with a six-inch serrated knife.

"Oh, hey there," he says, waving with the blade.

Mom's urn is just beside him, sitting on the workbench, pieces of the dead bird all around it.

"What are you doing?" I ask.

"Just cleaning it."

"Cleaning it? For what?"

"The bones. We're going to need the bones, Boo."

"Why?" I ask.

Dad looks over to the urn. "We need to tell her."

THIRTY
RICHARD

"What are you talking about?" Lacey asks.

I set the knife down and motion for her to come inside the shed. I wipe my hands clean on a rag and then pick up Kara.

"We can't, not yet. It may compromise everything," she says to me.

"Kara, we're knee deep here. We have to."

Lacey hesitates at the door.

I glance to her and meet her eyes. There's fear in them. She doesn't trust me, I can see it in there. I look back to Kara. "Let me tell her something. She deserves that much."

Kara is silent. I can't tell if she is thinking it over or just upset with me.

"Dad?" Lacey stays at the doorway. "I don't know what's going on." She chuckles nervously. "Not in here. Not out there. Nowhere, really. But we have a problem."

114

"What is it?" I reply.

"The rest of the vultures fell down. We have a massive pile of dead birds." She steps to the side and points them out in the yard. "They all fell in the front but I threw them back here before anyone saw them."

"Oh," I say as I see. "Excellent. Great work, Boo."

"Great work?" She laughs louder. "Dad, we're in big trouble here. You heard Deputy Thompson. If he sees any more dead animals you are going to be locked up."

"He didn't say that," I quickly correct her. "It doesn't matter anyway. If the birds are already falling then we are further along then I thought. It's almost over. Don't you worry, we'll be okay."

"How?" She throws her arms into the air. "How are we going to be okay? Giraffes and vultures are falling down dead in our yard. Things aren't going to be okay. It's getting worse, Dad. We're screwed!" She steps backward and lets the door close.

I hear her stomping away. I feel bad for not telling her more, but I trust Kara's judgment. She's been right about everything so far.

"Let her go," Kara says, as if she knows I was thinking about her. "We just have to wait a little bit longer. It's all going to be over soon."

"I know. I know."

I leave Kara in the shed while I retrieve the rest of the vultures. I stack them in a stinky, maggoty pile in the corner. I can see their rank blood staining the plywood floor already. I need to get them cleaned and disposed of tonight.

I finish off the first bird, dumping the feathers and rotten flesh into a plastic trash bag. I take the bones outside and spray them off with the water hose. I decide to leave them on the steps of the back porch to dry off, and then go back in the shed. I count the remaining birds, realizing I need to work faster if I am going to get it all done tonight.

THIRTY-ONE
LACEY

I pace the living room, checking the front yard. I'm looking for everything from more dead birds to Deputy Thompson, to Renee and those goons. Every time I see a clear front yard and an empty street, I do a silent 'thank you' in my head. I'm not a believer in god or some kind of a higher being, but it feels right to thank someone. I know we are on our last chance here. If the cops are called out one more time we'll be in deep shit.

After ten minutes of pacing, I go into the kitchen and wash my hands vigorously. I smell dead animals on them all the time now. The kitchen soap is a tropical flowery scent, but instead of masking the rotten bird smell, it just makes my hands smell like tropical death. I dry them off and grab a glass out of the cabinet. I fill it with tap water and take a long, slow swallow. When I set the glass down I see Dad out the window. He's setting bird bones on the porch. I shake my head, speechless. Sometimes I think he wants to get caught and taken away. At least then he won't have to deal with me.

I watch as he picks up the dead vultures two at a time and takes them into the shed. I'm guessing he's planning on taking them all down to the bones. I can't imagine what he thinks we need bird bones for. Whatever weird scheme he's plotting sounds like it will end with one or both of us going to jail.

I turn away from the window and head upstairs. I need to get my mind off things. My room feels small and suffocating. I'm not sure I can stay in here for long. I sit on the bed and try to focus on anything other than death and prison.

I see my phone sitting on the nightstand. It's plugged in, still charging. I go over to it and swipe my hand across. The battery is at ninety percent. Close enough. I pull it free from the cord and go back to the bed. I unlock it and see I have a missed call from Renee. *Bitch*. I have no desire to call her back. I also see I have a text from Tony. My heart stops for a second. I don't even remember giving him my number. In fact, I'm pretty sure I didn't give it to him. I read the text.

Sorry about the other day . . . I get weird sometimes.

I really like you . . . I want to start over again.

My hand hesitates on the reply button. I can't imagine him not knowing about the giraffes or my dad taking the urn everywhere. In a town like this things spread like venereal diseases. He must be playing coy with me.

But what if he isn't? What if he genuinely likes me? I'm not sure I have the time or space for another person in my life. I look around my empty room. Well, maybe I do. Maybe I have plenty of time and space. Maybe Tony is the exact distraction I need.

I decide to text him back.

It's fine. I like you too. Let's try again.

I sit and stare at my phone. He replies a minute later.

What are you doing tonight?

I can't help but smile.

Nothing.

He replies immediately.

Come to the corner store. I get off at 10. We can start over.

I text back.

See you then.

I stare at the phone for another few minutes. When he doesn't reply anymore I figure he must be busy at work and the conversation is over. Even though nothing has changed from five minutes ago, I feel better. I think this might be a good thing, despite how crazy my life is right now.

I click out of my messages and check the clock. It's only quarter to seven. I have some time to kill.

I think about food, but the tropical death scent on my hands makes my stomach waver in the wrong kind of way. Not that Dad will eat anything if I make dinner. Instead, I decide to take another shower. I don't want to see Tony smelling the way I do.

I pick some new clothes and lay them on the bed, then jump in the shower. The hot water feels amazing and I quickly find myself thinking about Tony. I almost laugh out loud how ridiculous it is that we started talking right now, in the middle of all this crazy shit happening. I'd been walking to that store, buying snacks and drinks, for over a year. Whenever Tony worked we would play a little game of flirty small talk, but it had never gotten past that. Yet now, when my mom is dead and my dad is losing his mind, when I have police threatening to take away everything I have left, that's when we decide to take it to the next step.

My life can't ever be simple.

As soon as I am out of the shower and dressed, I hear the doorbell ring. I put the hairbrush down and run to the door. My heart is thumping so loud I can hear it. As I'm descending the steps, all I can think about is Deputy Thompson arresting my dad. I picture him standing on the front porch with handcuffs dangling from a balled-up fist. I can see him staring me down, knowing I had lied to him. I wonder what my sentence will be?

When I open the door, Renee is leaning on the railing, chewing a thick wad of gum. Her bicycle is lying in the grass. After the initial shock of seeing her, I glance behind her, scanning the yard for more dead birds. The last bit of the sun is setting and it makes it hard to decipher shadows from objects lying in the grass.

Next door, I see Ms. Plume getting out of her car. She's dragging a black plastic bag up the driveway and into her garage.

"Hello?" Renee says. The tone of her voice makes my eyes twitch. She starts waving her hand in my face. "Earth to Lacey! Hello? Are you in there?"

I make eye contact with her. "What do you want, Renee?"

"I know your dad is insane, but I didn't know you were," she says, looking over her shoulder at the empty yard. "What the hell are you looking for?"

"Don't worry about it," I reply. "Was there something you needed or are you just here to annoy me?"

"The sheriff told me to keep an eye on you."

"You mean Deputy Thompson. He's not the sheriff," I correct her.

"Deputy, sheriff, whatever." She chomps on her gum with an open mouth. I can see the pink glob as it's squished repeatedly in her teeth.

"Well, aren't you special."

"I'm just saying . . . I saw your dad with the urn."

"Okay, and . . .?"

"And," she pauses for dramatic effect, "I saw him picking up a dead bird and taking it in the backyard."

"Yeah, a bird fell in the yard," I say. "What do you want him to do, leave it there?"

I can see her face as she realizes she doesn't have the smoking gun she thought she had. "Anyway, I just wanted to say that I'm keeping an eye on you two. If I see any more dead animals I'm calling the sheriff."

"You mean deputy."

"Whatever."

"Awesome," I reply. "Thanks for the heads up. Glad to know someone's got my back." I slam the door shut before she can say another word.

THIRTY-TWO
RICHARD

It takes me several hours to get all the bones of the vultures clean. I can feel my hands start to cramp as I pull the trash bag closed. I have to squish the rotten flesh and feathers down in order to tie the bag off. I don't even attempt to move it. I can tell it will weigh a ton.

"You did great," Kara says.

I look over at her. I can see her smiling at me. "Thanks. I don't know if I could have finished it if it wasn't for your company."

She stays silent.

I wipe my hands off and pick her up. "Let's go in."

I realize as I step out of the shed and into the dark backyard that I lost track of time. I shuffle onto the porch, avoiding the bones I laid out over the steps. I think about picking them up and taking them into the shed with the rest of the bones, but my body is aching. I need to rest.

When I get inside, the house is dark. Not a single light is on in any room.

"Lacey!" I call out.

"I think we've got the place to ourselves," Kara says.

I smirk and go into the kitchen, flipping the lights on. I set Kara on the counter and open the fridge. There isn't a thing to eat or drink. "She must've gone to the store to get some food. I keep forgetting about things like that."

"You've got a lot on your mind."

I go to the pantry and find a can of soup. I feel like I haven't eaten in days. The big lunch we had earlier only made me hungrier.

"At least your appetite is back," Kara says.

"You can say that again," I reply as I pop the can open and start digging directly into it with a spoon. I empty the can in a minute and then look for another.

"You're going to eat us out of house and home."

I push around old cans of beans and half-full bags of flour and sugar. There aren't any more cans of soup. "I think we're already out of house and home. Whatever that means."

We both laugh.

"Take me upstairs. I want to take another shower with you," Kara says.

I think she's rediscovered her passion. If I think back to the months of sickness and late night doctor visits, I realize, before this week, we hadn't made love in nearly a year. That explains why we suddenly can't keep our hands off each other.

"You don't have to ask me twice," I reply, scooping her into my arms.

THIRTY-THREE
LACEY

I used to love walking at night. I guess part of me still does, but right now, it feels like the night is suffocating me. There's a thick, heavy weight to it. I feel it on my shoulders and back. It's pressing down on my head, pushing in against my eyes.

I thought getting away from the house would make me feel better. I thought spending some time with Tony would help me forget everything. So far, it isn't.

I'm nearly to the corner store and I haven't thought about anything but Renee and her chewing gum. I wish I would have smacked it out of her mouth. I stop on the side of the road and quickly spin around, looking for her. I know she's following me, hiding in the shadows, sitting on her bike and watching.

"There are no dead animals here!" I yell out. I focus my voice, trying to send it directly toward a shadowy spot across the street. I don't see her there but it feels like the most logical spot she would be if, in fact, she is following me.

I squint, trying to see into the darkness, trying to determine shapes and depth. After a few seconds it feels pointless. I turn back to the corner store and head to the parking lot.

I decide not to go in. I don't want to be in the bright lights, not right now.

When Tony comes out, he's holding a bag of sunflower seeds. He tosses them at me. "Here, for you," he says.

I barely get my hands out of my pockets, catching it in a fumbling display of clumsiness. "Thanks."

"I don't want to rehash anything from last time, but I'm glad we're doing this," he says and then starts walking.

"It's fine," I say. "But if you see anything dead, just ignore it. I get enough of that at home."

"Absolutely."

We go for several minutes without a word. I think about opening the sunflower seeds, rubbing my finger on the plastic bag over the outline of one of the seeds. Finally, I say something to break the silence. "I used to like night walks."

"Not anymore?" he asks.

"Not lately." I don't look at him, but I feel his eyes on me. "I don't know if it's just part of growing up or just a part of life that I've somehow avoided until now. I think my parents sheltered me pretty well. Now that I'm basically on my own, I feel the weight of the world. It's crushing. Night walks seem to exacerbate that. At least, in my mind it does."

"You're alone with your thoughts."

"Exactly. Alone and suffocating under their weight."

Tony closes the gap between us. Our steps fall in line, shoes landing just inches apart. "You don't have to be alone," he says.

"Is that a pick up line?" I chuckle but then stop when I see he was being serious.

"I didn't mean it like that. I mean, I do, you know. I am interested," he says, stumbling over his words. "But I meant it like I'm here if you need to talk or need help or something."

"I appreciate the offer, but I'm not sure you can help me."

We walk silently after that. It doesn't feel like an awkward silence, more like a mutually agreed upon silence. It makes the weight of the darkness feel a little lighter.

When we get close to my street, I say, "If I told you something, would you promise not to freak out?"

"Of course not."

"No really. It's pretty fucked up. I have a feeling you're going to freak out."

"I won't. I promise," he says.

I'm not sure where to start. I try to begin a few different times, but keep stopping before a single word gets out.

He stares at me with an amused expression.

"Never mind," I finally say, then start walking again.

Tony reaches out and grabs my arm, stopping me. "I know about the giraffe thing. I heard about that a while ago. And I heard today about your dad taking your mom's urn for a ride in the front seat."

My mouth drops open. I knew it.

"Your friend told me about the urn thing earlier today at the store."

"Renee?"

"Yeah, I think that's her name. I'm terrible with names."

"She's not my friend," I say. "Did she say anything else? Anything about the police, or dead birds, or anything about me?"

"Police?"

I start to walk again. "It's complicated."

He stays beside me, falling back in stride. "I'd like to hear it from you, you know. Make sure what I heard wasn't all exaggerated rumors. If you still want to tell me."

"I'm sure you get the gist of it," I say as we get in front of my house.

"I'm not freaking out. It's all pretty hard to believe, but I'm not freaking out. You don't have to run inside."

"Hard to believe, eh?" I grab his arm and pull him down the driveway.

"Where are we going?"

"My backyard," I say. I lead him to the fence, opening the gate, and drag him into the backyard.

The moon is just a sliver, stabbing through a cluster of clouds. It makes the yard so dark the dirt mounds on top of the graves look like deep, black holes. It looks like we live on a minefield.

"Okay, this is a little weird but I don't see any dead giraffes," Tony says.

"It doesn't come until morning."

"So why are we here now?"

"We're having a sleepover."

"In the backyard?"

I lead him to the porch, nodding to the two plastic lawn chairs sitting up against the house. "We can stay up here."

He stops when he sees bones scattered across the steps. "Uh."

"Freaking out yet?" I step over them and sit down on a chair.

"Not at all," he says, smiling. "Well, maybe a little." He sits down next to me, still staring at the bird bones. "Are those giraffe bones?"

"Vulture. There were like a dozen of them," I say. "I think the rest are in the shed, or else my dad buried them earlier."

I think I hear him swallow as he looks across the yard again.

"So you want me to stay here with you until the giraffe shows up?"

"I tried staying up all night once before, but I fell asleep. I still have no idea how or when they get here. When we wake up they're here." As soon as the words leave my mouth I wonder if telling him all of this is a bad idea. I feel like I can trust him, but if he freaks out and runs to the police we're in deep shit.

"I guess I'm in," he replies. He takes out his phone and starts texting someone. Before I can ask, he glances at me and says, "Telling my parents I'm staying at a buddy's house."

"Such a good kid," I tease.

We spend the next several hours talking about everything from books and films to growing up in town. We both find it strange that we lived so close to one another but didn't meet until he started working at the corner store. I suppose I wasn't much for social events and since he's a couple of years older than me, it wasn't likely we would've run into each other at school. The more I think about it the more it starts to make sense. I wonder how many people are living in this town that I wouldn't recognize if I bumped into them.

The night feels like it goes by in a flash. We are so busy getting to know each other neither one of us pays any attention to the time. It's not until the first hues of pink break across the sky that we realize it's nearly six in the morning. I quickly glance to the 'spot' in the yard the previous carcasses were and see the latest.

"When? How?" The words fall from my gaping mouth.

"Shit!" Tony says. He stands up and goes to the rail, rubbing his weary eyes. "It really happened."

I get up and stand next to him, shaking my head as I look over the rotten animal. "Right in front of us. It came out of nowhere. No one is dropping it here. No one is throwing it out of a plane." Deep down I've known it was happening like this the whole time, I just couldn't wrap my head around it enough to believe it fully. But now, now that I'm standing here and I know it just appeared out of nowhere like some shitty magic trick, I feel like we are in even bigger trouble than ever.

THIRTY-FOUR
RICHARD

"You look beautiful in the morning light," I say. "You always have."

"We have work to do. Today will be a long one," Kara replies.

"I guess that's a no to morning sex."

I see her eye me up and down. "I suppose we can squeeze in a quickie," she says.

I lean in for a kiss, caressing the side of the urn. She feels so soft and smooth. Just as my lips touch down, I hear the sound of shovels striking the dirt. I stop and tilt my head toward the window. There's no doubt in my mind it's the sound of digging.

"What's wrong?" Kara asks.

"I think Deputy Thompson found our graveyard." I pull on a pair of jeans and open the bedroom door. I see Lacey's door open, but don't think much about it. I quickly run down the stairs, leaving Kara in the bed.

When I get downstairs I go straight for the back door, flinging it open and stepping onto the porch. I immediately stop.

"Oh hey, Dad," Lacey says.

She's holding a shovel, standing beside a young boy about her age. He's in the middle of digging when he hears her and stops. I don't recognize him, but he nods to me.

"What's going on?" I ask.

She motions to the latest giraffe carcass. "I thought we'd get a head start and dig the hole right away. Tony can only help for a couple of hours, might as well get some hard labor out of him." She smirks at him as she says the last part.

"Who is Tony? Where did he come from?"

"He's my friend."

"Okay." I'm not sure what to say. She doesn't have many friends. I don't want to yell at her. "But don't dig anymore, at least not right there. I'm going to grab my shirt and shoes. We have a change of plans today."

"Change of plans?"

"You'll see. I'll be right back." I run inside and back up the steps. I find an old shirt and pick out some socks.

Kara watches me silently from the bed.

"I think Lacey has a boyfriend," I tell her, sitting on the edge of the mattress while I pull on my socks. "She's got him out there digging."

"I want to meet him."

I grab my shoes from under the bed and slide them on. "Fine, but we need to figure out what we're going to tell them. Lacey should know the truth."

"We only have to tell her what she needs to know. And we don't have to tell her friend anything."

It feels wrong leaving Lacey out. I don't understand the point of it, but I trust Kara's instincts. I know everything will be okay in the end. I hope so, at least. I pick her up and we go downstairs. Before going outside, I stop in the kitchen and turn on the coffeemaker. I know I'll need it.

When I go back out, Lacey and Tony are standing by the porch, examining the vulture bones. Tony has a skull in his hands.

"Pretty cool, eh?" I say.

He pinches his face, eyeing the urn. "What's that for?"

I hold her up, pushing her out toward him. "This is my wife, Lacey's mother, Kara. Kara, this is Lacey's friend, Tony."

Tony looks at Lacey. "Is this for real?" he asks her.

"Freaking out yet?" she says.

I put Kara down on the porch railing. "There's coffee brewing, should be done in a minute," I say as I walk past Lacey and her friend. I go to the shed and check the other vulture bones, before grabbing the chainsaw and my knife.

"What's the change? Why don't you want us to start digging?" Lacey asks from the doorway.

"Oh, you can dig," I say. "Just not any more empty graves."

"I don't understand. Where are we going to dig then?"

"It's starting sooner than we thought. Your mom says we only have a couple of days left. We need to get the bones back up."

She shakes her head. "You want us to dig up the old graves and get the dead giraffe pieces out?"

"Yes," I reply as I walk by her.

"What are all the bones for? What's happening in a couple of days?"

I start up the chainsaw, acting like I don't hear her. I know I'm not supposed to say anything else yet. She asks again, but I rev the engine and move into the giraffe carcass, cutting into the rotten flesh.

THIRTY-FIVE
LACEY

"Dad? Dad?" I yell but he keeps cutting into the giraffe. I think about tapping him on the shoulder, make sure he knows I'm talking to him, but then rotten flesh starts spraying into the air. I have to jump backward to avoid getting covered in it.

Tony is watching my dad from the porch. Even though he's saying he isn't freaking out, I can tell from his expression this is more than he was expecting.

I go over to him. "Let's get some coffee," I say and grab his hand. We step around the vulture bones and go inside the house.

"Dude," he says as soon as the door is closed. "Your dad is like completely insane."

I go over to the cupboard and pull out three mugs. I fill them up with the fresh coffee. "I know it's a lot to take in." I hand him one of the mugs.

"I'm taking it in just fine," he replies. He takes a tiny sip and sets the mug on the table. "I know insane when I see it. The giraffe thing is pretty crazy but it's a different kind of crazy. I'm not sure I'll ever understand that, but your dad . . . the bones and the urn thing. I really think he's lost it. I think everyone is right. I think you're both a little off."

I'm stunned. My immediate reaction is to shout, scream at him that he's wrong. I'm fine and my dad is fine. We aren't insane. I want to punch it into his face. We . . . Are . . . Not . . . Insane. I take a long, slow sip of the hot, black coffee. When I've calmed down, I set the mug on the table. "I guess that's fair. You don't really know either of us. I took a chance and invited you here. I realize that's a mistake now. It's too much for you. I get it. I just thought you were different."

"Fuck," he says and starts pacing the kitchen. "I'm sorry. I like you, I really do, but this is fucked up." He points out the window. "Your dad is chopping up a dead giraffe right now. He thinks your mom can still hear him from inside the urn."

"Actually," I say, "he thinks the urn is my mom. He sees her body instead of the urn."

"That's worse," Tony replies. "And you're just like okay with this?"

"Okay? Do I look okay with it? My life is a fucking disaster. I know how screwed up it is, but right now I have no choice but to dive into the crazy and make the best of it. I thought having you here would make it easier but I can see that I was wrong. Go on. You can leave."

"I wish I could dive in with you. I had a great time last night. It's been a while since I had a conversation like that, but all of this," he says, motioning to the backyard again. "This is too much."

"Got it," I say. I feel my eyes swelling, but try to swallow the hurt back down. I pick up my coffee and take another long swig, composing myself in the process.

He finally stops pacing and looks at me. I guess he's waiting for a better response, but I've got nothing else left. After a minute of nothing but the sounds of a chainsaw slicing through giraffe flesh, Tony walks away. He leaves through the front door. I'm not sure if I'll ever see him again.

I hold back tears, gulping the coffee, feeling it scald my throat on the way down. I pick up Dad's mug and take it out back. I see the concerned look on his face when he sees me alone, but he doesn't stop cutting.

"Lacey?"

I think I hear my mom's voice. It's hard to tell over the sound of the buzzing chainsaw. I look at the urn, slowly taking a step closer to it.

"Mom?" I lean into the urn, almost touching my ear to it. All I can think about is how Tony may be right. Maybe I'm crazy too. Maybe we are all losing it.

"Lacey?"

I stand upright, realizing the voice isn't coming from the urn at all. It's coming from behind me. I spin around and look to the fence. The top of Ms. Plume's head is jutting above the fence. I can just see her eyes above the wooden planks. Her tiny hand raises up and waves me over.

I set my Dad's coffee mug on the railing next to the urn and head over to the fence. Something tells me this isn't going to be a friendly hello.

"Lacey," she says again, and this time I'm far enough from the chainsaw that I clearly hear her.

"Hey, Ms. Plume."

"I just wanted to say goodbye."

"Are you leaving?"

"In a way, I suppose."

"What do you mean?" I ask.

I think she stands up on her tip-toes because she rises up a few inches, high enough that I can see all of her face. I do the same and we are almost face-to-face.

She points over the fence, back toward my dad. "That's going to be the last one, I think."

"What? The giraffe?"

"Yes."

"How do you know?" I ask.

"I saw the birds falling. I remember what your mother said. It's almost time."

"Did she say anything about what would happen to her when she died?" I didn't feel comfortable telling her my dad thought she was somehow living as the urn.

"I'm sure she made it to heaven. She was a lovely woman," Ms. Plume says. "Don't you worry about that. As for me, well I guess I'll find out pretty soon."

That last part threw me off a little. I can't imagine why she would think of herself as evil in any sort of way. She was a sweet old lady.

"Tell your father that I got the missing pieces, just like your mother wanted. I don't have the strength to get them out for you, but I'll mark the spots today. I wish you and your father the best of luck. Goodbye," Ms. Plume says and walks back to her house.

I stand silently for a moment, confused by the words of the old lady. I want to ask her what she's talking about but I don't even know where to start. Instead I call out to her, "Goodbye, Ms. Plume."

She doesn't look back.

I walk back over toward my dad. He stops the chainsaw, setting it on the ground. "Dad?" I ask.

He turns to me, smiling. "Yes?"

"Where should I start?"

He points to the closest dirt pile. It's the oldest grave. I pick up the shovel and start digging. I remember when Dad first dug it. I remember how terrified I was, how confused I was then. I suppose I'm just as confused now as I was then, but it's at a whole new level. Instead of dwelling on it and freaking out, I decide to do my best to ignore it. I dig hard and fast, working my arms and legs vigorously. I think I'm becoming my dad.

THIRTY-SIX
RICHARD

Lacey has been digging for an hour straight. She hasn't taken a single break, not even when I sat on the porch with Kara and drank my coffee. I'm proud of her, buckling down and working hard. I know it has something to do with that boy. I have a feeling they had an argument earlier, probably about the dead animals. I can only imagine how it looks to someone on the outside. I want to go comfort her, tell her everything will be okay. Honestly, I don't know for sure. But what I do know is that we have a lot of work to do in a very short period of time. The more we ignore the outside influences, and hopefully have them ignore us, the better a position we'll be in.

I don't waste any more time chopping up the carcass. Instead I get my serrated knife and start removing the flesh from the bone. It's a long process, but the more I do the better I become. Soon enough I've got a pile of cleaned bones.

"Dad!" Lacey calls out.

I finish plucking off a few stubborn pieces of cartilage and go over to the grave she's standing in. "What's up?" I ask.

"Look!" She holds up a femur bone. It's already clean, not a single spot of flesh is left on it.

I glance back at Kara, wondering how it's possible. Somehow she knew. She's always known. When I turn back to Lacey, she's pulling another clean bone from the dirt, shaking the loose soil away.

"Another," she says.

"That will certainly make things easier," I reply. "Try to get them all out, if you can."

She nods and goes back at it, tossing the two she already found on the ground beside the grave.

I go back to the carcass pieces and continue cleaning them. Before I know it, Lacey is climbing out of the hole, holding the giraffe skull. I watch as she runs her hand over the stubbed horns protruding from the top of it. The thing looks completely intact, down to the very last tooth. She finally sets it with the others and grabs the shovel.

"Hey," I call out just as she is about to strike the next mound of dirt.

She stops in mid-air and looks at me. "Yeah?"

"You can take a break if you want," I say. "Get a bite to eat or something."

"Dad," she says, motioning to the yard of dirt mounds. "We've got so much more to do. I can't stop yet."

I want to tell her we have time, she doesn't have to kill herself, but I'm not so sure. I just nod, letting her get back to it.

We work into the night, only stopping for water and bathroom breaks. I finish cleaning off the latest carcass and dig up three of the buried ones. All of them were just like the one Lacey found: nothing but skeletons. I know logically it's impossible for them to have gone through the decomposition process that quickly, especially buried and away from the elements, but I don't dwell on it. However it's happening, it's a good thing. I realize there's no way I would have been able to get all the carcasses cleaned in time.

I look up at Kara again. She's just as confident as she's always been, eyeing me with a sly smirk that makes me wonder just what she's capable of doing now. *Stick to the plan and everything will be okay.* Her words repeat in my mind.

When it gets too dark to see, I get Lacey up out of a grave. "We need to make a run to the hardware store," I say as I grab her hand and pull her up.

"What for?"

"Lights, for one. I can't see anything out here anymore. We also need some cement."

"Cement?" she asks, dusting dirt from her pants legs.

"You'll see."

THIRTY-SEVEN
LACEY

When we get back from the hardware store we unload all the bags of cement and the new wheelbarrow. Dad sets up a tripod stand with dual thousand-watt lights. It shines over the majority of the yard, mimicking daylight conditions.

Before we get started, we sit on the porch and finish off some fast food we grabbed on the way back. I didn't think I'd be able to eat, but as soon as I take the first bite I feel famished. I devour the burger and fries in just a few minutes.

Dad sits near me, but keeps his attention on the urn. I want him to open up to me. I want him to tell me what's really going on. Why are we collecting bones? Does he know why the giraffe carcasses started coming and where they are coming from? I can tell he knows more than what he's telling me. And why the fuck is he so convinced the urn is Mom?

Calm down. I can't let myself get worked up.

"Dad? What's really going on?"

He looks over at me like he forgot I was still here. Instead of answering honestly, he glances back at the urn.

"Dad?"

When he turns back toward me he avoids eye contact. "It'll all be over soon. I can't tell you more than that."

"The bones? The cement? I don't get it."

He stands up, crumpling his bag of food. "You'll have to trust me. You'll find out everything soon."

Again with the vague answers. I'm trying my best here. I don't know how much more I can take. I feel so alone.

Dad stands up and gets back to work. There are two more graves to dig, two more piles of giraffe bones to exhume. He starts on one and I know he is thinking I'll be behind him, digging up the other, but whatever was driving me earlier is gone. My body is feeling it and I don't want to move. I've been awake for close to forty hours by now.

I sit reflecting on everything for a few minutes: Mom's death, Dad's insanity, the giraffes, the vultures, Tony, and even Ms. Plume. I remember I'm supposed to tell Dad about the missing pieces or something. I wonder if it means anything or if it was just the crazy ramblings of an old lady on the verge of losing her own mind. It takes all I have left just to stand.

I move past Mom's urn, eyeing it suspiciously. Even though I know it's nothing but a metal vase filled with ashes, it gives me the creeps. When I get close to Dad, he's already two feet in, digging just as fast as ever. The man never tires.

"Dad," I call out.

He stops shoveling and looks back to me, raising his eyebrows.

"I think I'm going to bed. I can't do it anymore."

He nods, half smiling as he says, "Goodnight, Boo."

I stand there for a second, watching him drive the spade into the dirt and tossing the soil away. Until he has more answers for me, I can't bring myself to help him bury dead animals and then dig up their bones. I can't be a part of this insanity any longer.

I turn and go inside.

After a quick shower, I change into sweats and curl up in bed. I feel so disconnected from the outside world I think about logging into social media but know it's an endless descent into wasted time. I pull out a paperback from my bookshelf. With nothing but the lamp light on, I start reading a cheesy horror about rabid cats. It doesn't take long until I'm dozing off. I close my eyes and think about Tony.

The sound of laughter wakes me. I see Tony and Renee. They're lying in bed next to me. They're both naked, kissing each other, giggling between each wet liplock. I see their tongues lapping and slurping. Tony breaks away from her mouth and glances at me. His eyes run over my body and I realize I'm nude and fully exposed. I quickly pull the blanket up, covering my naked body. Both he and Renee start laughing again, mocking my embarrassment.

Then Renee raises her eyebrows at me, smiling slyly as she moves down Tony's chest and stomach, going all the way down to his cock. She shoots me a knowing look as she takes it into her mouth.

I try to scream out. I try to tell them to leave but my voice is lost. Only silence passes by my lips.

After a minute of oral pleasure, Tony lifts her head and then lays her back on my bed. He gets on top of her and starts fucking her right beside me. Both of their eyes are on me, staring at me as they go at it. I keep trying to scream out for them to stop. I try to tell them how much I hate them both and want them to leave. All I can hear is the sound of their laughter.

I shut my eyes and will myself to wake up. This must be a bad dream. It has to be. When the sound of their laughter suddenly stops, I open my eyes. Tony and Renee are gone, replaced with my naked dad. He's thrusting his cock into a woman with large bouncing breasts. Her head is an urn.

I sit up in bed, shaking and sweating. I look back and see I am alone. Worst fucking nightmare of my life.

I rub my eyes, noticing the early morning light coming in through the window. I pick up my phone and check the time. A few minutes after six. I lie back onto the pillow. I'm still tired, exhausted really, but after that awful dream I have no desire to try sleeping again.

My mind races back to last night. I left dad out there alone, digging up bones and doing something with cement. As curious as I am to figure out what he's doing, I just want to think about something else. Anything else but giraffe bones and digging graves.

I replay the conversation I had with Tony the other night in my mind. It was nice to be able to escape everything like that, to just sit with a guy and talk about things that didn't involve my fucked up life. I miss him. I wish he hadn't left like that. I wish he wouldn't have freaked out over everything.

I chuckle out loud, realizing how ridiculous I sound. Of course he freaked out. My dad is a lunatic. My entire life is a mess. What the hell was I thinking inviting him to my house? I was the crazy one, thinking I could have any type of relationship in the middle of everything that was going on. My frustration level reaches a boiling point. Dwelling on Tony isn't helping anything.

Shit, my head is a swirling wreckage. I can't focus on anything that isn't chaos. I need answers.

I decide to get up and get dressed, then I'll start with Ms. Plume. Old people are always up early. And if she is planning on leaving for good, I need to catch her before she leaves.

THIRTY-EIGHT
RICHARD

It took the entire night, but I was finally finished. Kara's encouragement was the driving force. That and the knowledge that I had no more time. She seemed confident today was the day. The day we had been planning for since her death. The day she told me she saw in her dreams after getting sick.

I never asked her how it would happen. I never asked how the dead giraffes or the dead vultures came like they did. I trust her. That's all I need.

"How's it look?" I ask.

Kara smiles at me. I can see she is proud. "Almost there."

"Almost?"

"There are a few missing pieces. We'll need them to ensure its stability. They're important," she says.

"I used every bone we had. Every single minuscule piece from every giraffe and vulture skeleton. There are no more pieces left."

"I had someone else help. I knew it would be too much to ask of you, so I asked a friend to help out with the other pieces."

"A friend?" I rack my brain trying to think of who she could have asked. "Who?"

"Ms. Plume."

Right as she says the name I hear a scream. Before even registering what Kara had told me, I react, realizing immediately the scream came from Lacey. I run, dropping everything and leaving Kara behind.

It was way too early for Lacey to be outside, she rarely ever got up this early, but it definitely sounded like it came from out front. I race out the gate and scan the yard. I don't see anything right away, but then Lacey comes stumbling out of Ms. Plume's house. She hops down the porch steps and falls over in the grass, crying out.

I run over and drop next to her, wrapping my arms over her back.

"What's the matter? What happened?"

She mumbles incoherently, pointing to the house.

"Did something happen? Are you hurt?"

"No, Dad. Not me," she says through sobs.

"Look at me." I lift her head, pushing her hair away from her face. "What happened?"

She rubs her eyes with the back of her arm and then points again. "It's Ms. Plume."

"Show me," I say, helping her to her feet.

Lacey moves slowly but she comes along. When we get to the front door I can see the lights are all off. The curtains are drawn and block out most of the morning light. But after a few steps inside I see the silhouette of a dangling body. There is a slight sway, nothing extreme. It almost looks like a peaceful hanging.

Lacey stays back at the door, still crying.

I walk inside and up to the body. Ms. Plume has a noose tied around her neck. The rope is strung through a self-made hole above the doorframe that separates the living room from the kitchen. Lying on the floor near her is a hammer and chunks of drywall. A turned-over chair is a few feet behind her.

I look at her face and see her eyes, bulging and bloodshot. Her tongue hangs from her mouth. The color of her skin is off. She's wearing a floral dress with a pair of fuzzy purple slippers that somehow managed to stay on her feet.

I turn to Lacey. "She's dead," I say.

"Dad!" She goes back outside.

"What? What did I say?"

When I get out there Lacey is sitting cross-legged on the grass. She's still sniffling but the sobs have ended. I go and sit next to her.

"Dad?"

"Yeah, Boo." I rub her back.

"What did Mom tell you about Ms. Plume?"

"Not much. Why?"

"I think Mom told her everything. She knew about the giraffes."

"I think everyone in the neighborhood knows about the giraffes," I say.

"I'm serious, Dad."

"Your mom did tell me something. She said Ms. Plume was helping us."

Lacey looks up at me. "Helping how? Last night she told me she had the missing pieces. She said she would mark them all for us."

"Kara said we needed more pieces and Ms. Plume was the one getting them for us. That's all I know. I don't know where they are. I don't know what they are. And I don't know why she would kill herself. I do know that we need to find those pieces right away. We only have a couple of hours left."

"Left until what?"

"Let's find the pieces and take them back to our house, then I'll talk to Kara about filling you in. I think it's time you heard the truth. But first things first, we need those pieces," I say.

We get up and head toward the front door but Lacey stops short.

"I can't go back in. I'm sorry, Dad."

"It's okay. That's fine. You stay right here and I'll do the looking, okay?"

"Thanks."

I go back inside and search the entire house. I can't find a single bone anywhere. I'm not sure if I'm looking for horse bones or dog bones, or something even more obscure. When I'm sure the house is bone-free, I go into the backyard. I walk from fence-line to fence-line. There aren't any dirt mounds or disturbed areas of lawn. There's nothing in the tiny shed or under the deck. I can't find any trace of bones and I definitely don't see any marked areas. I finally go back around to the front yard.

"Nothing," I say.

"Are you sure?" Lacey asks.

I lift my empty hand into the air. "Not a trace."

THIRTY-NINE
LACEY

My life is death. Death in hospital beds. Death in funeral homes. Death in urns. Death hanging from ropes.

I'm not sure I can handle any more death, but for some reason, I feel like this is just the beginning.

"Not a trace," Dad says.

I think about my conversation with Ms. Plume. When she told me goodbye, I thought she was leaving. I thought I would never see her again. I didn't know she meant she was killing herself. I can't imagine why she would want to do it. It must have something to do with my mom. Something about the missing pieces.

"She said she marked them," I say to Dad. "You didn't see any markings?"

"Nothing."

I tried to think of where she would put them, where I would

put them if I were her. It came to me quicker than I expected.

"Dad, the empty lot next door!"

We ran there together, crossing our front yard and darting into the overgrown grass next door. Before we were halfway in, something in my backyard caught my eye. It was enormous, towering above the privacy fence, nearly as tall as our two-story house. It looked like it took up the entire length of our backyard. I stopped and stared at it, moving my eyes over every piece, taking it all in. Circular corners, arching windows, spires, and even a weird battlement that wrapped around the top of the first level.

"They're here! I see the markers!" Dad shouts.

When I don't respond, he comes back and stands beside me.

"Did you hear me? They're here!"

My eyes are still locked on the thing towering above us. "Dad, that's a . . . you built a . . ."

"It's a castle," he says. "I built us a castle."

"It's made of bones."

"Giraffe and vulture bones, and whatever is in these marked graves that Ms. Plume made for us. Kara says these are the last pieces."

"You did all of this last night?" I ask.

"Yes. But I couldn't have done it without your help."

"Dad, there's no way the cops aren't going to notice this. The whole neighborhood is going to be calling the police on us."

"We better get these last pieces dug up and put on before they wake up then," he says. "I'll go grab the shovels, you stay here."

I'm still staring at the ridiculous bone castle as he leaves. I can see each individual giraffe bone. I can see each vulture skull cemented onto the other bones, somehow all stuck together and holding. I realize that, of all the fucked up shit I've seen in my life, this is by far the most fucked up of them all. My dad really is a psychopath.

"Here," he says when he returns. He hands me a shovel. "Come on. We don't have a lot of time."

The graves are small. Nowhere near what we made for the giraffes. Each one is marked with a large red X spray-painted directly on the dirt. Seven in all. Dad kicks his spade into the loose soil, digging into the red dirt. I start on a different one, working without realizing what I'm doing. My mind is racing so fast I can't focus on any one particular thing. The images are going by in blurry streaks, unidentifiable as anything but colorful smudges. Despite feeling dizzy and barely coherent, I continue to dig.

It doesn't take us long to reach something. Ms. Plume didn't bury them deep. Dad pulls out a large, black plastic bag, just as I finish digging mine out. He holds it up, brushing off the clinging dirt.

"I guess I'll open it here, see what we're dealing with," he says.

I pull the bag out of my grave and set it on the ground, then watch Dad. He tears the bag open near the top, unable to untie it. He reaches his hand in, shifting things around and then hesitates.

"What is it?" I ask.

After a few seconds, he lifts out a skull. A human skull.

I jump back, moving away from the bag in front of me.

"Lacey, wait!" he calls out.

I drop the shovel and turn, running before he can stand up. I don't run home, I run down the road. I have no idea where I'm going, but I need to get away. I need to get far, far away.

My feet stomp onto the pavement, clopping down hard with each heavy step. I run for nearly a mile until the panic subsides and I feel semi-normal again. I feel the sun shining on my back and head. I glance over my shoulder and see the rays breaking through tree branches. It's still low, still early. I also check and make sure Dad isn't following me.

It's clear behind me, but when I look in front again, I see a figure walking down the road. They are still pretty far ahead, but I can tell they are heading toward me, on the same side of the road. I immediately slow down, though refuse to stop running. I move at a slow jog, staring down the person, willing them to disappear. It isn't until I am nearly upon them that I recognize the walking figure.

"Tony!" I say as I nearly run into him.

He grabs my arms, stopping my momentum. "Lacey? What are you doing? What's wrong?"

I struggle against him, trying to wrench my arms free, but he holds tight.

"What happened? Tell me what happened?"

Finally I stop fighting him and collapse into his chest. He releases my arms, embracing me with his. I look up at him, panting and out of breath. "Why are you walking down the street this early?" I ask him.

"I just asked you the same thing."

I pull out of his embrace and stare at him accusingly, remembering the awful things he said about me. "You answer first," I say.

"Melissa, the older lady you met that works third shift, called out. I had to pull a double. I had to work from two yesterday afternoon until six this morning. I was on my way home."

"That sounds awful."

"It was. Now, you? Why are you running? What happened?"

I try to start the explanation but no words seem to describe the situation properly. I stumble each time.

"It's your dad, isn't it?" he says.

"It's not just my dad. It's everything. My neighbor killed herself. I found her body this morning."

"You're like a magnet for dead things." He smirked as he spoke, but I could tell he wasn't joking.

"The past few weeks have felt like that."

I explain how I feel, purposely leaving out everything about the human bones. Before I know it, we are walking back toward my house. I tell him about my mother, about how she used to be. I tell him all the silly childhood memories I have of the two of us together before she got sick. I even tell him about the months of doctor visits and hospital stays. I recount the entire process up until her death. And when I finish I have tears running down my face.

"Sorry," I say. "That all just kinda slipped out."

"Nothing to be sorry about. I'm glad I could be here for you."

I meet his eyes. "You mean that? I mean, even after all the craziness?"

"Yeah," he chuckles again. "You are definitely the nuttiest chick I know, but I don't know, I like you."

"Thanks, I think."

I hear sirens in the distance, sounds like they're coming up from behind us. Tony and I turn together and spot the barrage of speeding cars and flashing lights as they appear. We quickly step off the road and onto the grassy shoulder. I count the cars as they fly by. One, two, three, four, five, six, seven. Something serious is going on.

"You don't see that every day," Tony says.

"Never around here," I say, realizing my house is less than a mile away. I step on the road and start walking again just as two firetrucks come blaring down past me, riding the horn and scaring the shit out of me.

"Where do you think they're going?" Tony asks, looking both ways before getting on the street next to me.

"I know exactly where they're going. Come on."

FORTY
RICHARD

I decide not to chase after Lacey. We don't have time. According to Kara, everything is happening today and I still need to get the new bones in place. I let her go.

It takes me longer than I want to get all of the bags uncovered. I toss each one over the fence and into our yard to keep from looking too suspicious. Then I grab the two shovels and circle back around the house to the castle. On the way around I see a woman walking her dog. I wave a hello, but her eyes move away from me and to the bone castle in the backyard. She stops and stares. I quickly run around back and start opening all the bags.

After only a few minutes I get the quick-dry cement mixed and the human bones set in place. Just as I am starting to feel like I actually pulled this off, I hear police sirens. All I can think about is Deputy Thompson taking Lacey away.

"Don't worry about them," Kara says. "They're too late."

I set my tools down and run to one of the front windows. "Are you sure? I don't see anything."

"Lock up the doors, it will be starting in minutes."

"Lacey isn't back yet," I tell her.

"Where is she?"

"She ran off, it was becoming too much for her."

"We don't have time for this. She needs to be here."

"I know." I watch the road, hoping Lacey will return. Instead, several police cars stop in front of the house. "Shit."

I see Deputy Thompson get out of one of the cars. He puts one hand on his holster, but doesn't pull the pistol out. His eyes are taking in the enormous structure. None of the cops approach the house or even the backyard, they all seem too stunned. The neighbors are filing in behind them. I recognize Lacey's friend Renee. She is sitting on her bike. A few other kids gather near her. Everyone is pointing and staring at the bone castle.

Then I see her—Lacey—and her friend. I try to remember his name but it escapes me. Trevor, maybe. I don't recall. They run through the crowd and try to get to the house but the police stop them. I can't tell what anyone is saying from up here.

"It's starting," I hear Kara say. "Look at the sky."

The clouds come in fast, blacking out the sun. The entire sky darkens into a strange purple. Thunderclaps echo across the treetops and between the houses. I feel a vibration in the bone floor.

"Are you sure we're safe here?" I ask.

"Trust me."

"I do. I do."

FORTY-ONE
LACEY

"Let me go!" I shout. "That's my house!" One of the cops has his chubby arms around my waist.

"Let her go," I hear Deputy Thompson say. He steps in front of us.

The chubby cop releases me.

"Where's your father at?" Deputy Thompson asks.

"Where do you think?"

"In that . . . thing?" He nods to the castle.

"I guess so. I haven't been home."

"What is it?"

The sky darkens. Clouds rush in on the heels of rumbling thunder. The trees start swaying as cold gusts descend. We all look up when the sun suddenly goes out, turning the morning light into something dark and stormy. I take the opportunity to run by Deputy Thompson. I'm already to the gate before he sees

I'm gone.

"Wait! Stop right there!" he calls out.

I get through the fence but stop just on the other side, not because of Deputy Thompson, but because of the moat. I realize I hadn't been out back since the castle was built. I had no idea he dug a deep trench around it. Dark, brown water sits inside, the wind rippling the surface into tiny waves.

"Dad?"

A huge door creaks open. It looks like a collage of bones in the shape of a standing rectangle. My dad smiles at me.

"Where have you been?" he asks. "It's starting!"

I motion to the stormy sky. "You think?"

Dad pulls a ladder out of the castle and lays it across the moat. "Climb across!"

I look around for Tony, realizing I left him out front. When I don't see him, I get down on my hands and knees and crawl across the ladder straddling the brown, stinky water. He helps me up and pulls me into a short-lived hug, releasing me when Deputy Thompson comes running into the backyard. Dad pulls the ladder back across the moat and inside the castle.

"Go on in," he says.

"Stop! We need to talk!" I hear the deputy shout, but Dad closes the bone and cement door, locking it.

I look around at the inside. Every wall, every floor, every inch of the place is either bone or cement. Some of the bones I recognize and can tell they came from either a giraffe or a vulture, but others I'm not so sure of. It's kind of amazing, in a weird, sick way. "Dad, what's going on? What's happening out there?"

"Let's go upstairs."

He shows me to a staircase and we go up to the second level. I see my mom's urn sitting on the kitchen table from our house. The whole upstairs is like a mock house. There's a little kitchen area and a sitting area. I have no idea how he was able to do all of this overnight.

"We know we should have told you earlier," Dad says. He sits down beside the urn.

"We?" I glance out a window. I can see the police and all the neighbors. They're still out there. Some are watching the sky, while others are looking up at the castle. I turn back to my dad. "When are you going to stop with the urn thing?" I grab my mom's urn off the table before Dad can stop me. I move it to the window, threatening to drop it.

"What are you doing?" Dad asks. He stands up but doesn't come forward.

"It's for your own good," I tell him. "She's gone, Dad. You can't talk to mom." I feel something inside the urn. It feels like something is moving, the weight of it going from one side to the other. It's almost liquid-like. "Did you get water in it?"

"Lacey, please. Just listen. Listen and you can hear her. It's Mom. I promise you. It's Mom."

"Listen to what? I don't hear voices like you do. I don't hear her."

"Kara, it's time," he says. "Tell her."

After a moment of silence, I feel nothing but pity for my dad. He's gone completely insane. I get ready to drop the urn.

"Lacey, please just listen. Your mother explained everything to me. First the dead giraffes, then the birds, then the people.

Everyone out there is going to die."

I look back outside. Everyone is still standing around.

"It's just a bad storm. No one is going to die. We have to go, Dad. The police are going to come in here and arrest you. You have to give yourself up."

"I believe Kara. The dead will rise. Everyone out there will be dead by morning."

"The urn told you this?" I ask, shaking the thing out the window.

"Don't drop her!"

I see the pain in my dad's eyes. He really thinks it's her.

"Kara! Please! Tell her!"

I start to loosen my grip.

"Boo," Mom says softly. "I'm here."

My head whips around to the urn and I nearly drop it out the window. My knees shake and I fall backward, letting the urn tumble to the castle floor. I back away, crawling until I hit a wall.

Dad swoops in and picks up the urn. He hugs it and kisses the top, cradling it like a child.

I think I've officially lost it. When I stepped through the threshold of this fucked up bone castle I must have walked right into crazytown.

"Lacey, it's okay." Dad holds out a hand for me but I refuse it.

"No, Dad. It's not okay. I heard her. I heard her voice."

"Of course you did," Mom says.

I can hear her perfectly. It's her voice. There's no denying it. "How?" I'm shaking. Tears are swelling in my eyes.

"I had to be here to make sure this got built. I had to make sure the two of you were safe," she says.

Dad glances out the window. "It's a mess out there. The things are everywhere."

"So it's all true? Everything is true?"

"Yes," she replies.

"Why didn't you talk to me sooner?"

"I had to wait until you were ready. We needed to make sure you were here and safe. Your father is right. Everyone out there will die."

I suddenly remember Tony and jump to my feet. I run to the window. "We have to let Tony in. We have to save him too."

Dad wraps his arms around me. "It's too late for him."

I look out the window. At first it looks like everyone is still standing around talking or watching the storm clouds. I think I see Tony talking with Renee.

"I'm so sorry, Boo," Dad says in my ear.

I rub the tears away from my eyes and look again. This time it's complete chaos. Everyone is running or fighting. Rain is falling in sheets. Thunder and lightning beckon back and forth. Skeletal people are moving around the crowd, attacking them. I see Deputy Thompson getting his face ripped from his skull. I see the dead things tearing limbs off kids. I see two rotten men eating into Renee's stomach. Then a third bites her neck, nearly severing it. Finally, I spot Tony. He's on top of a police car, trying to kick the dead away, but there are too many of them. The things surround him and pull him off, piling on as he hits the ground. I think I hear him screaming as they start eating. When I've had enough, I turn from the window.

"There's nothing we could have done," Mom says.

I see her sitting at the table. Dad is standing beside her, holding her hand. I look around for the urn but can't find it anywhere. I meet her eyes. It's really her. She's back!

"Mom!" I run over and collapse into her.

FORTY-TWO
RICHARD

I can't help but smile, despite the carnage taking place outside. I watch Lacey hug her mother tighter than she has since she was a child. It feels right. It feels like we are whole again.

While they are still embracing, I go to a back room. I dig through one of the boxes I brought and find the old boombox. I think they'll get a kick out of this. I take it back to the kitchen area and set it up on the counter, checking to make sure the batteries are still good.

"Dad, what are you doing?" Lacey asks.

I flip it on and push the CD player to play. A mix of eighties new wave fills the castle with electronic synthesizers and bouncy beats. I reach out and pull them both up from the chair.

"I feel like dancing," I say.

Both of their faces light up as we hold hands and dance like the world outside is ending.

About the Author

J. Peter W. currently resides in Richmond, VA.

Other than writing, he loves graphic design, gardening, and spending time with his family.

When he retires, he plans on building an elaborate labyrinth in his backyard filled with strange statues and weird animatronic figurines. You will be invited!

For more information visit: www.jpeterw.com

Other **Atlatl Press** Books